"Maybe you ca **because all th Europe got to your airline tick**

"How's your knee, K___?"

"I bet they even chased you onto the plane. My knee hurts like hell," he said cheerfully. "But if we walk any slower I'll be tempted to kiss you again. You were dynamite in the daytime. I hate to think what you'd be like by moonlight."

"That's only sex," Nell said testily.

"Nothing wrong with sex."

How would she know? "One more thing," she said with considerable determination. "You take the bed, I take the chesterfield."

"Don't want to talk about sex, Nell?"

"Do shut up, Kyle."

"How bored all those men in Europe must be without you," Kyle murmured.

Although born in England, **Sandra Field** has lived most of her life in Canada; she says the silence and emptiness of the north speaks to her particularly. While she enjoys travelling, and passing on her sense of a new place, she often chooses to write about the city which is now her home. Sandra says, 'I write out of my experience; I have learned that love, with its joys and its pains, is all-important. I hope this knowledge enriches my writing, and touches a chord in you, the reader.'

Recent titles by the same author:

AFTER HOURS
HONEYMOON FOR THREE

SEDUCING NELL

BY
SANDRA FIELD

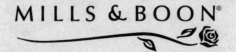

MILLS & BOON®

First published in Great Britain 1997
Harlequin Mills & Boon Limited,
Eton House, 18-24 Paradise Road, Richmond, Surrey TW9 1SR

© Sandra Field 1997

ISBN 0 263 80224 8

Set in Times Roman 10½ on 11¼ pt.
01-9708-54452 C1

Printed and bound in Great Britain
by Mackays of Chatham PLC, Chatham

CHAPTER ONE

"OH," NELL cried, "just look at the view! Please, Wendell…can you stop for a minute?"

"It's only the barrens," her companion said. "Nothin' much to look at." But, obligingly, he put his foot on the brake pedal and the ancient truck wheezed to a halt.

Nell opened the door, which squealed a metallic protest, and slid to the ground. Dumbstruck, she gazed around her.

I've come home, she thought. This is where I belong.

Although it wasn't the first time in the past two weeks that she had had that thought, it was the first time it had struck her with such intensity. Newfoundland, island province off the east coast of Canada, had captured her imagination and her heart from the moment she had stepped off the plane in St. John's and filled her lungs with cool, fog-swept air that smelled of the sea. The spell had woven itself around her tighter and tighter every day that had followed. And now she was totally its captive.

Somehow I've got to stay here. I don't know how. But somehow.

She couldn't go back to Holland and pick up the placid threads of a life that could have taken place on another planet, so remote did it seem, so alien to the woman she had become in just two short weeks.

Wendell cleared his throat noisily. "You ready to go, missie? I got to get to the coastal boat in Caplin Bay on time to unload this stuff."

Nell turned around, the sunlight twined in her chestnut hair. Wendell's age was anything from seventy up, and his clothing in a state of disrepair that more than matched his truck. But his bright blue eyes twinkled in a way that she was sure would have been quite irresistible in a younger man; and for the past three hours he had regaled her with hair-raising tales of ghosts and smugglers and shipwrecks. She said impulsively, "I'm going to stay here for a while—just let me get my gear out of the back."

"Stay? What for?"

Because it's so beautiful that I could die happy right now? Because I'll do anything to delay the moment I have to get on the coastal boat in Caplin Bay and go to Mort Harbour?

She said lamely, "I want to take a few pictures—it's so pretty."

"Hell of a place in winter." Wendell scratched at his whiskered chin. "Don't feel so good about leavin' you here, missie. This ain't St. John's, you know. Not much traffic on this road so as you'll get another ride."

"I'm used to hiking. Besides, I've got my tent and I always carry food with me. I'll be fine." She flashed him a quick smile, hurried around to the back of the truck and wrestled with the lobster twine that kept the backboard in place. Then she hoisted her pack onto her back and retied the knots. Feeling the heat reflecting from the pavement, she walked to Wendell's window and held out her hand. "Thanks so much, Wendell. I really enjoyed meeting you. Perhaps I'll see you again when I reach Caplin Bay."

"I hangs out there quite a bit. You take care now, missie." He shook her hand with surprising strength, winked at her and, in a clash of gears, headed down the road. The truck belched a farewell puff of black smoke. The rattle of the engine diminished in the distance. Nell moved to the gravel shoulder of the road and looked around her.

They had been climbing steadily through scrub forest

until Wendell had turned the last corner. Spread all around her were the barrens—rounded outcrops of granite surrounded by low shrubs and licked by the pink foam of bog laurel. Delicate tamaracks huddled in the hollows. The afternoon sun glinted on the scattered ponds, turning them into gold coins tossed with a profligate hand over the landscape. The silence was so intense as to be almost a presence in itself.

Nell took a deep breath, filling her lungs with the clean, sweet air. She couldn't go back to Holland. She'd smother there. Maybe, just maybe, when she got to Mort Harbour, she'd find a welcome...

A slight movement caught her eye. She turned her head. Where the rocks rose to a peak against the horizon on her left, a caribou had just stepped into the open.

She had been told it was rare to find caribou here in summer; they tended to migrate to higher ground in an effort to escape the flies. Her heart tripping with excitement, she crossed the road and carefully traversed the ditch. Caribou, she also knew, were relatively tame. With luck, she could get a closer look. Even a photograph.

The barrens had looked smooth and inviting from the road. But Nell had been in Newfoundland long enough to know that the smoothness was deceptive and the invitation a mockery; walking anywhere past ten feet from the highway could be extraordinarily difficult. Especially when laden with a heavy backpack. The first hollow she came to, she shucked off her pack and tucked it among some scrub spruce out of sight of the highway. After unzipping her smaller haversack, she loaded it with her camera, a couple of apples and her water bottle, and took off again. Her boots gripped the granite, slithered over clumps of wet grass and plunged into the dark brown peat, which sucked hungrily at her heels. She stopped to apply repellent, and saw with a jolt of pleasure that a

yearling had joined the other caribou; Nell's binoculars
brought it so close she could see the tag ends of leaves
hanging from its blunt muzzle.

Slowly, Nell lowered the binoculars. She was standing
knee-deep in rose pink laurel blossoms. Flecks of mica
in the granite sparkled and shone like tiny jewels; a sparrow was piping its small, clear song from a wizened
spruce nearby. For a split second, she became a part of
her surroundings, engulfed in a wave of happiness so
pure it was as though she was bathed in the gold of the
sun.

The moment passed, but the memory of it was hers.
With a sigh of repletion, she counted a third caribou as
it ambled into the open. It was a cow, like the other
adult. Nell scrambled over a series of outcrops and
jumped from rock to rock across a puddle. All three
caribou had stopped to graze. She edged closer, keeping
hidden from them as much as she could, until she
reached a clump of feathery tamarack near enough to
give her an excellent view. Crouching down, she made
a seat for herself by a granite boulder and stretched out
her legs, focusing the binoculars. Across the barrens
drifted the click of caribou hooves; she was convinced
she could even hear the animals' jaws munching on the
dry lichens. Their coats were glossy with health, the hair
a blend of thick cream and a lustrous dark brown. Like
café au lait, she mused, smiling to herself.

Time passed. Nell munched on an apple and took a
couple of photos. And then, from the dark ribbon of the
road, she heard the distant murmur of an engine. The
vehicle that appeared was a cross between a Jeep and a
van. To her intense annoyance, it slowed, pulled over
and came to a halt. She saw light glint from what could
only be binoculars.

She tucked herself lower, thankful that she was hidden
from sight. Scowling, she watched the driver get out and

stretch. A man. She didn't want to share her solitude with a man. She didn't want to share it with anyone. Maybe once he'd had another look through his binoculars, he'd be on his way.

Instead, he shut the van door so quietly she didn't hear the sound and headed across the road toward the caribou. Even from her faraway perch, she could see that he was limping slightly.

Go away, she thought fiercely. Get lost. Go to Caplin Bay, or Drowned Island, or St. Swithin's. But don't come here.

A sparrow flitted into a nearby shrub, momentarily distracting her. Rather horrified, she discovered that she was glowering at the man as though he was her mortal enemy. She wasn't normally so antisocial. But then, nothing had been normal ever since that day, late in May, when she'd decided to clean up the attic of the house in Middelhoven where she'd grown up. In an old trunk pushed against the chimney, she had found a diary belonging to her grandmother, Anna, a shadowy figure whom she only remembered meeting once, long ago, when she was a little girl. She'd taken the diary downstairs and had sat up late that night reading it from beginning to end.

Only two months ago. It felt like a lifetime.

The man, Nell was glad to see, was struggling with the bog and the underbrush just as she herself had. Unfortunately, if he kept going in the direction he had chosen, he would end up tripping over her. In these vast stretches of wilderness, where people were so few and far between, it seemed a supreme irony that an intruder should shatter her peace and happiness. Damn him anyway, she thought vengefully.

He was closer now, near enough that she could hear the crackle of twigs from his passage and the rasp of his boots on the rocks. He was wearing jeans and a dark checked shirt, his sleeves rolled up to the elbows. His binoculars were slung carelessly over one broad shoulder. With a faint twinge of unease, she noticed his height, the strength latent in those shoulders and the grim lines of his face. No moment of perfect happiness for him. He looked like he was on his way to the funeral of his best friend.

She had to do something. She couldn't let him fall on top of her. Not with that face. Definitely not the kind of man to find a chance meeting on the barrens amusing. She tensed, bracing her knees to stand up, wondering if she should clear her throat to warn him of her presence before she spoke.

And then he solved the dilemma for her. His foot slipped. He lurched forward, grabbing for the slender trunk of the nearest tamarack, his involuntary cry of pain raising the hairs on the back of her neck. As she instinctively twisted to help him, he began to swear, with quite astonishing virtuosity, in French.

His jaw was tight, and Nell could still see the deeply bitten lines of pain around his mouth. But her sense of humor, which had gotten her into trouble on more than one occasion, managed to ignore these symptoms. She half stood up and demurely, in French, added a couple of very crude expressions that she had learned in her younger days in Paris and that he had omitted.

The man whirled. Before she had time to even croak a protest, she found herself slammed on her back against the granite boulder, his body pinning her so hard that the rock dug into her spine. His hands bit into her shoulders, his face only inches from hers. His eyes were blazing like those of a man demented.

He's mad, Nell thought blankly. Out of his mind. I've come all this way to be murdered by a psychopath.

But Nell hadn't roamed Europe on her own without learning a thing or two; and she had never been one to lie down tamely to fate's blows. Fueled by a mixture of sheer terror and adrenaline, she brought her knee up to his groin with lightning speed.

The man's body wasn't there. Her knee knifed empty air.

Before she could strike again, he had hauled her roughly to her feet, shaking her as if she were of no more account than a carpet to be beaten. With a truly impressive degree of rage, he snarled, "What the hell do you think you're playing at, sneaking behind a tree like that?"

She should have said something conciliatory to calm him down. Rule one. Don't fight back. Shoving against his chest with all her strength, Nell seethed, "Are you a raving maniac? How dare you attack me like that! I wasn't sneaking—I was watching the caribou."

"You little idiot! I could have killed you."

He was still shaking her. She might as well have been yelling at the caribou for all the effect she was having, she thought furiously, and kicked him hard in the shins. "Let go!"

The toe of her boot connected with bone. He swore again—in English this time—his voice as rough as the granite against which he had flung her. But then, mercifully, he stopped shaking her, although his fingers remained clasped around her shoulders. In all honesty, Nell was just as glad, for she wasn't sure she could have stood upright.

He took a deep breath and said flatly, "Hell and damnation."

Nell stayed very still, watching as the light of sanity returned to eyes so dark a blue as to be almost black, feeling the shudder rip through his body as though his frame were her own. Her anger vanished, and with it her terror. Briefly, the man closed his eyes, swallowing hard. His shoulders sagged so that she felt the weight of his hands on her shirt. The weight and the warmth, a warmth that was oddly disturbing.

He was no madman. Of that she was sure. Although she couldn't have said where that certainty came from.

She said with a lightness that very nearly succeeded, "It seemed a pity that you'd left out a couple of quite effective swearwords. French can be so expressive, can't it? And I really was about to stand up and speak to you when you fell."

His eyes flew open, all his anger rekindled. "Goddammit, do you have to remind me?"

"Goddammit, do you have to yell at me?"

"You're yelling, too!"

"Little wonder," she snorted.

The sun was slanting across her face, shadowing her cheekbones and her straight nose, dusting her skin with gold. He took another of those deep, shuddering breaths; his eyes were roaming her face as if he had never seen a woman before, as if he was striving to commit each one of her features to memory.

Nell stood very still, shaken by the intimacy of his gaze, feeling as if every secret she had ever held was exposed to him. Then he said quietly, "When I was a kid, we used to pick bunches of blue-eyed grass to give to the teacher. Have you ever seen it? The flowers are like little stars that are blue and purple at the same time. Your eyes remind me of them."

"Oh," said Nell, feeling her cheeks grow warm and trying very hard to repress the knowledge that he was easily the most attractive man she'd ever come across. Although that admirably succinct North American word "hunk" would express her opinion far more accurately.

With an exclamation of self-disgust, the man dropped his hands to his sides, and the mood was shattered. "You saw the caribou from the road, too. That's why you were hidden."

She had forgotten about the caribou. Glancing toward the bluff, she whispered, ''They've gone.'' Across her face flitted regret and the memory of that moment of shining happiness.

He said heavily, ''I scared them when I fell.''

Her nostrils flared. ''I expect you scared them when you jumped me. A starving wolf's got nothing on you.''

''There aren't any wolves in Newfoundland.''

''A bear, then,'' she said pettishly.

''Bears don't starve in the summertime.''

There was a gleam of humor deep in his dark eyes. ''Hunk'' also began to seem a very wishy-washy concept. Devastating? Gorgeous? Sexy? Any or all of the above? Nell said, ''It might be nice if you could bring yourself to apologize. I don't usually expect total strangers to wrap me around a chunk of granite and then shake me out like an old rug.''

''Yeah...''

As he hesitated, Nell saw that any approach to humor had fled from his features. It was interesting that ''handsome'' wasn't one of the words she had come up with, she mused. His face was too rough-hewn, too individual for mere handsomeness. Too used, she added thoughtfully. Hard used. Ill-used. And for rather a long time, unless she was mistaken.

He said in a staccato voice, ''I—hurt my leg a couple of months ago. I've done very little hiking since then. It drives me nuts when I fall down like a two-year-old.''

''Real men don't trip over rocks?''

''Real men can at least stand on their own two feet!''

Lines of frustration had scored his face from cheek to chin. His mouth was clamped shut. He had a beautiful mouth. Nell said hastily, ''Keep going—apologies at some point are supposed to include that ordinary little phrase, 'I'm sorry.'''

"That's why I was angry," he snapped. "I've just explained it. What more do you want—a diagram?"

"That may indeed have been why you were so angry," she snapped right back. "But it doesn't explain why I'm going to have bruises all over my back tomorrow morning."

"*Are* you French?"

"I'm from Holland. Don't change the subject."

"You speak English extremely well," he said suspiciously.

"Hooray for me. Are you with the CIA? Is that why you jumped me? Or do you fancy yourself as the next James Bond?"

"No wolves in Newfoundland and no CIA, either. What the hell would they want with this chunk of rock?"

"So you're a policeman."

"I am not. *You're* the most persistent and inquisitive female I've ever met."

"Only because you're avoiding the issue," Nell returned pleasantly. "Out of interest, do you go around attacking everyone you meet? Or do you just pick on women who are smaller than you?" It was difficult to see exactly how tall he was because of the uneven ground, but he definitely topped her five feet eight by several inches.

He ran his fingers through his hair: thick, wavy hair, worn a little too long and as dark as peat. As dark as the caribou fur, Nell realized with an inward shiver and hurriedly continued her survey. His nose was slightly crooked, he could have done with a shave, and there were frown lines in his forehead that shouldn't have been there. No wonder she hadn't considered him merely handsome, Nell thought, and waited for his reply.

As if the words were being pulled from him one by one, he said, "For the past few years, I've been in some rough places. The kind of places where you act first and ask questions afterward. You startled me. I didn't even take time to think.'' His smile was more of a grimace. "So I immobilized you instead.''

"You sure did.''

His eyes narrowed. "You even speak like a Canadian. Are you sure you're Dutch?''

"I first learned English from a Canadian couple who lived in the village where I grew up,'' she said shortly. "I'm still waiting.''

"What for?''

"How about this? Petronella Cornelia Vandermeer, I'm extremely sorry that I terrified you witless and I apologize for acquainting you so intimately with a granite boulder. That'd do for a start.''

He held out his hand. "Kyle Robert Marshall.''

His handshake was firm, his palm warm, and she could lose herself in those midnight blue eyes. She said, tugging at her hand, "I'm called Nell.''

As though the contact had freed something in him, Kyle added, "I'm really sorry, Nell. I must have scared you.''

She stopped tugging, letting her palm rest in his. "The word 'psychopath' did cross my mind.''

Although his laugh was rueful, it made him look years younger. "You reacted pretty fast yourself.''

"Just as well you moved.''

He grinned. "Just as well, indeed. I'd have been singing soprano for the rest of my life.''

His voice was a rich baritone. Nell pulled her hand free and said with careful restraint, "A mosquito has just landed under your left ear.''

He brushed it away. "I left my repellent in the van.''

"I've got some.'' Nell bent to her haversack, passed him the little plastic bottle and found herself watching his every move as he smoothed the liquid over his throat and arms. In the course of her work, she'd met a lot of

men from countries all over Europe. Sophisticated
Frenchmen, sexy Italians, devastating Norwegians,
hunky Hungarians. But never one to pull her to him as
instinctively as this man pulled her.

As he passed her back the bottle, Kyle said, "Where's
your car? I didn't see it on the road—one reason why
you took me by surprise."

"I don't have one. I was hitching a ride."

He frowned. "On your own?"

She looked around. "No one else here. Besides, didn't
you tell me there aren't any wolves in Newfoundland?"

"Newfoundland is not peopled entirely by saints."

"You sound like my father," Nell flung back, then
instantly wished she'd kept her mouth shut.

"Don't tell me how to live my life—is that the message?" As she nodded, he added softly, "Trouble is, I'm
used to giving orders. And used to being obeyed. So I'll
drive you wherever you're going, Petronella Cornelia.
As a rather more concrete way of apologizing."

"And what if I say St. John's?" The capital city was
an eight-hour drive from the barrens.

"You were headed south if you got out when you first
saw the barrens. The options are therefore limited.
Caplin Bay, St. Swithin's, Salmon River, Drowned
Island…that's about it."

She liked matching wits with him, Nell realized
breathlessly. "Where are *you* going?"

"Caplin Bay."

She bit her lip. Wendell had been going to Caplin Bay
and now Kyle was. Maybe it was time she went there,
too. After all, she didn't have to take the coastal boat
for Mort Harbour right away. She could camp in Caplin
Bay for a couple of days. Try to plan some kind of
strategy.

With a sense of taking a momentous step, she said,
"I'm going to Caplin Bay, too."

"Good," Kyle said briskly. "Let's go."

But as he half turned away from her, putting his weight on his left knee, it buckled under him. His features convulsed; his harsh intake of breath echoed in Nell's ears. She grabbed for him, bracing herself against the nearest rock, aware for the second time of the lean length of his body. As though he resented her help, he pushed himself upright and shook free of her.

"Say it," Nell said. "You'll feel better."

"You don't let up, do you?" he said nastily.

"Would you rather I had hysterics? Or fluttered around you doing the helpless-female act?" Nell wrung her hands, batted her lashes—which were thick and dark and one of her better points—and simpered, "Oh, Kyle, where does it hurt?"

He gave a reluctant laugh. "Okay, okay. Unfortunately, I've used up my entire stock of French. And my mother'd be horrified if she ever found out I'd sworn at you in English."

"German can be very expressive. I'll teach you, if you like. Sounds to me like you could use a few more good cusswords."

Gingerly, Kyle placed both feet on a patch of smooth granite and straightened to his full height. "For once, we're in complete agreement."

"We have all the way to Caplin Bay," Nell said. He was over six foot, broad shouldered and narrow of hip. Dark hair, dark brows, dark eyes, and a dark past, too, unless she was very much mistaken. If she was smart, she'd head for St. John's and not Caplin Bay. Then, uncannily, he responded with a similar train of thought.

"You know what? I can't say I've ever met a woman quite like you."

"My mother always said I was mouthy."

Something must have shown in her face. He said gently, "Is she no longer living?"

"She died four months ago."

"I'm sorry."

He had invested the phrase with genuine feeling. She wouldn't cry. Not here. Not now. Not in front of a stranger. "Let's go," she muttered.

"Perhaps you could use a few of those cusswords yourself." As she glanced up, her eyes liquid with unshed tears, Kyle took an awkward step toward her, brushing her lids with his fingers, then smoothing her hair back from her face. "You have beautiful hair," he said thickly. "Where it catches the sun, it shines like copper."

Quite suddenly, the level of emotion was too much for Nell. She tilted her chin and said, "It's awful hair—dead straight and too fine. That's why I keep it bundled up."

He said evenly, "It's beautiful hair, Nell."

As he tucked a strand into her braid, his fingers brushing her neck, she couldn't hide her involuntary shiver of response. Terrified for the second time in their all-too-brief acquaintance, she said meanly, "Guess what? The wolf's just made a reappearance in Newfoundland."

He flinched, and with bitter regret she knew she had cheapened his gesture beyond repair. He said in a hard voice, "Let's get the hell out of here. You go first."

And don't offer to help... He hadn't said that, but he hadn't needed to. The look on his face had said it for him.

Nell adjusted her haversack over her shoulder and clambered out of the hollow where the tamaracks were waving their feather-green branches in the breeze. Not even looking around to see if Kyle was following her, passionately wishing her words unsaid, she headed for the little stream that she'd crossed on the way up.

CHAPTER TWO

As NELL tramped along, she could hear Kyle following her across the barrens. Why should she be surprised that she had reacted to him with such terror? Hadn't her mother spent years instilling a fear of men in her?

Not men, Nell. Sex.

With the result that Nell, who was twenty-six years old, who loved a good party and who had dated men all the way from France to Italy, was still a virgin.

Scowling, she clumped her way through the laurel and Labrador tea, blind to their beauty. Her virginity, so old-fashioned, so anachronistic, was a close-held secret. Probably still would be when she was eighty, she brooded irritably, swatting at a mosquito on her wrist.

"Nell—look at the eagle!"

Startled, she turned around. Kyle was several feet behind her, pointing into the sky. She looked up and saw a great dark wingspan outlined against the blue as the eagle rode the thermals, its tail and head as white as the scattered clouds. She found the bird in her binoculars, almost certain she could see the hooked golden bill, and a few minutes later heard Kyle join her. She let the binoculars drop and looked right at him. "I'm sorry, Kyle," she said. "I shouldn't have made that crack about wolves."

Absently, he rubbed his left thigh. "It was a cheap shot."

"Mmm...nothing like sighting an eagle for making one's shortcomings obvious."

He grinned at her. "Let's agree on something. I'm not a psychopath and you're not a bitch."

She hauled out her water bottle. "I'll drink to that." She took a big gulp and passed him the bottle. As he tipped back his head and drank, she let her eyes wander from his throat muscles down his chest to his taut belly, then the length of his legs in their faded, close-fitting jeans. Beware, said her mother's voice. He's as beautiful as the eagle, Nell thought. And quite possibly as wild. "How's the knee?" she asked in a carefully neutral tone.

"It's been better." He passed back the bottle. "Thanks, Nell."

"I could lend an arm, you know."

"I can manage."

The grimness was back in his face. She didn't know what it meant and already she hated it. "Are there many eagles around here?" she asked.

"They're making a comeback, yeah."

"It's the first one I've seen—thanks for pointing it out."

She picked out what looked like the easiest way back to the road and started out again, going more slowly this time. Ten minutes later, she dug her toes into the gravel of the ditch and was back on the tarmac.

She turned and held out her hand; after the briefest of pauses, Kyle took it, and she hauled him up the slope. He was rubbing his thigh again, tiny beads of sweat at his hairline. She said brightly, "Sunsets must be spectacular here."

"You don't have to be so damned tactful," he grated. "Where's your gear?"

She had been so intent on Kyle's footsteps behind her that her backpack had not once crossed her mind. Blushing, Nell muttered, "I forgot about it—I'll be right back."

A few minutes later, they were on their way. True to her promise, Nell taught Kyle a number of rather choice words in both German and Dutch, told him about her work as a translator and about some of the contracts she'd been getting with large multinational corporations. It wasn't until they were winding down the hill toward the small cluster of houses that was Caplin Bay that she realized she had talked a great deal about herself and knew nothing more about Kyle other than that he was a very fast learner of foreign swearwords and a very good listener.

Quickly, she looked around. The village curved around the bay, where a sturdy wharf jutted into the sea; to her great relief there was no sign of the coastal boat. The headland at the far end of the bay was edged with a gray stretch of beach. She'd camp somewhere down there. "Could you drop me at the grocery store?" she asked.

"Aren't you staying at the bed-and-breakfast?"

"No. I'll camp."

"Nell, it's Saturday night—do you think that's wise?"

Wiser than staying in the same place as you. "I'm traveling on a shoestring," she said patiently. "I can't afford to stay at bed-and-breakfasts."

"At least let me buy you a hamburger at the takeout. Which is the nearest thing to a restaurant in Caplin Bay."

"It's nearly six. I have to get groceries and I need to get settled in."

"You sure are stubborn. How long are you staying here?"

She wasn't going to tell him about Mort Harbour. "Oh, a day or so," she said vaguely.

His eyes narrowed. "You don't want to see me again—that's what you're trying to say, isn't it?"

If she was to borrow one of his favorite words and tell the absolute truth at the same time, she would say that he scared the hell out of her. "I don't know why you're so angry," she said. "We met by chance, I don't know the first thing about you, and now we're going our separate ways. No big deal."

And whom are you trying to convince, Nell? she mocked silently. Kyle or yourself?

He pulled up in front of the grocery store, his tires skidding in the gravel. Banging the ball of his hand against the wheel, he said, "Is that what you want? That we never see each other again?"

What she wanted was to be transported miraculously into her unknown grandfather's living room in Mort Harbour. Into his living room and into his heart, she thought painfully. That was her priority; after all, hadn't she traveled thousands of miles and used up all her savings just to come face-to-face with Conrad Gillis? So the time wasn't right for any other emotional complications. And if there was one thing she was sure of, it was that Kyle Marshall could very easily become a major complication.

If he hasn't already, a little voice whispered in her brain.

"That's what I want," she said steadily.

He undid his seat belt and twisted so he could look right at her. His expression was unreadable. "You're right, of course," he said. "Absolutely right. I'm too old to be blathering on about eyes like flowers and hair like spun copper—and you're much too sensible and level-headed to read anything into a chance meeting on the barrens. Besides, you must be used to more sophisticated men than me. You did mention multinational corporations, didn't you? I'm sure if you can swear in five languages, you've done other things in five languages, too." He gave her a smile that was nothing but a movement of his lips. "Goodbye, Nell. The next time I need a good swearword, I'll think of you."

Before she could guess his intention, he leaned over,

gripped her by the shoulders and kissed her hard on the mouth.

His face had swooped down on hers, and there was no tenderness in the pressure of his lips. He's like the eagle, Nell thought dizzily. A predator...and then she stopped thinking altogether. Because while Kyle might have begun the kiss from some male need to assert his will, he didn't stay in that place for long. One of his hands buried itself in the soft mass of her hair; the other cupped her cheek, smoothing the line of her jaw. From a long way away, she heard him mutter something against her mouth. Then his lips were stroking hers, back and forth, again and again, with an exquisite gentleness that made nonsense of all her mother's strictures.

She felt as flushed as the laurel, as free as the eagle. She felt as she'd never before felt with a man: as though she was most truly herself. With a moan of sheer pleasure, Nell wrapped her arms around Kyle's ribs and kissed him back. His hand left her cheek to pull her closer to his body, and he deepened his kiss with a fierceness she more than matched.

A piercing whistle split the air.

Wrenched from a place that was as new to her as the barrens and more beautiful by far, Nell opened her eyes. Kyle pulled his mouth free. They both looked around.

They had gathered an audience. A teenage boy produced another earsplitting whistle, his female companions giggled, and from the window of his disreputable old truck, now parked beside them, Wendell was grinning at them. As she gaped at him, he gave her a thumbs-up signal. If she hadn't even heard Wendell's truck pull up, Nell considered ruefully, she was really in a bad way. Then she began to giggle helplessly herself as Kyle methodically went through every single word she had taught him on the drive to Caplin Bay.

She laughed until she was in tears; she laughed until

her ribs hurt; and she laughed all the harder as Kyle's affronted stare gave way first to a wry grin, then to a deep belly laugh of his own. "You do realize," she gasped, "that I now have to walk into that store and buy hamburger and dish detergent? Even the girls at the cash register were staring at us."

"Good," said Kyle.

"You've ruined my reputation in Caplin Bay and all you can say is good?"

"Yep. I haven't had so much fun in a dog's age."

Neither, if truth were told, had she. She said severely, "Unlock the back hatch, Kyle. I've got to get my gear out."

"Want to change your mind?" he said. "Supper at the takeout and a night at the bed-and-breakfast? Best offer you'll get all day."

The reckless gleam in his eyes was beguiling, and even to contemplate a night at the bed-and-breakfast with Kyle set Nell's heart racing. She said, "Are you kidding? After that kiss? When I'm so sensible and lev- elheaded?"

"You didn't like my calling you that?"

"I hated it," she said pithily. "Coming to Newfoundland is the most irresponsible and crazy thing I've done in my entire life. Push that button thing that unlocks the hatch, Kyle."

"Is the old guy in the truck another of your con- quests?"

"He drove me to the barrens and I don't have any conquests. Goodbye, Kyle."

"He and I will have to exchange notes," Kyle said, pushing the knob by the dash that released the hatch. "I bet he knows a swearword or two. Goodbye, Petronella Cornelia Vandermeer."

Somehow she hadn't expected him to let her go with- out more of a struggle. Without another of those dev-

astating kisses? Is that what you wanted, Nell
Vandermeer? Feeling thoroughly out of sorts, she scrambled to the ground, gave herself the satisfaction of slam-
ming the door as loudly as she could and got her pack
out of the van. Easing it onto her back, she marched
straight through the group of teenagers, daring them to
say anything.

Wendell was lounging against the doorway to the grocery store. "Didn't take you long to find yourself another drive," he cackled.

"He's not half as cute as you," she responded ami-
ably, and pushed open the door.

She bought a minimum of groceries, and when she
went back outside there was no sign of either Wendell
or Kyle. She trudged along the road toward the headland
and, with the ease of practice, found a campsite among
the trees just up from the beach, then made her supper
over her little one-burner stove. The sun had already
sunk behind the point. The sea was lacquered in apricot
and gold; seagulls drifted lazily homeward. The little
cluster of houses looked very peaceful.

Nell herself didn't feel at all peaceful. Her vision was
sharp enough to have picked out the blue sign in front
of a bungalow on the hillside: the bed-and-breakfast
where Kyle was staying. She didn't want to think about
Kyle. She didn't want to think about Mort Harbour, either. All she wanted to do was go to sleep and wake up
in the morning to a whole new day.

There should have been nothing especially difficult
about that plan. But although Nell curled up in her sleeping bag inside her tiny yellow tent as soon as it was
dark, it took her a long time to fall asleep.

Wendell's truck was roaring right in her ear. Roaring as
loudly as if the accelerator were stuck.

With a gasp of dismay, Nell sat bolt upright, her head

skimming the slanted roof of the tent. The roaring was
real, not part of a dream. All too real. So were the yelling
and the snatches of song, the beams of light piercing the
walls of the tent then vanishing, the flicker of flames
through the thin yellow fabric.

She rubbed her eyes, crawled out of her sleeping bag
and unzippered the tent flap. A full-scale party was in
progress on the beach. The roaring and the beams of
light came from three all-terrain vehicles that were spew-
ing out sand as they tore up and down the beach. The
singers were grouped around a campfire. With a sinking
of her heart, she saw that the party was entirely male.
Ten of them, counting the ATV drivers. Ten men and
several cases of beer.

Her tent was visible from the beach. Even though it
was—she checked her watch—nearly three o'clock in
the morning, the party showed no signs of abating. She
didn't need her mother's voice to tell her that the combination of beer, drunken males and loud machines was
not a particularly trustworthy one.

Praying that they wouldn't notice the outline of her
body through the tent, Nell hauled on a sweatshirt and
jeans, laced her boots and gathered up her haversack and
jacket. Then, at the last moment, she bundled her sleeping bag under her arm. She'd go farther along the headland and find a dry place under the trees where she'd
feel safer.

As she crawled out of the tent, one of the headlights
caught her full in the face, blinding her. A chorus of
voices began yelling at her, drowning the soft swish of
the waves. "Hey, baby, come and join us…Lotsa
beer…C'mon, sweetheart, we'll show you a good time."

No thanks, Nell thought, and headed up the hillside
into the trees, stumbling over roots and rocks because
she didn't have her night vision. As she looked back
over her shoulder, she saw with a quiver of fear that one

of the men was staggering up the beach toward her tent, brandishing his beer bottle at her.

Nell hurried deeper into the woods. Although the men sounded like happy drunks rather than mean ones, she had no desire to put their good nature to the test. Not at three o'clock in the morning. She shoved her way through the thickly interwoven spruce trees, remembering that she'd seen a pathway along the ridge, glancing back nervously to see if she was being followed.

With a suddenness that drove the breath from her body, she collided full tilt with a man who had just stepped out from behind a gnarled pine tree. She tried to scream, felt a hand clamp over her mouth and began, futilely, to struggle. She should have headed for the road, she realized wildly, not the woods, and did her level best to claw his face with her nails.

"Nell, stop! It's—" She struck out again, wriggling with the desperation of terror, trying to get a purchase with her boots so that she could lunge free. "Quit it—it's Kyle!" the man gasped.

Her ribs were cinched by her captor's arm, forcing her to stillness. The timbre of his voice struck a chord in Nell's memory, freeing her from the knife-edge of panic. His voice wasn't the only thing that was familiar. At a more primitive level, so was the clean, masculine scent of his body. She jerked her head up and looked straight into deep-set eyes as black as the night. "Kyle?" she whispered.

"Yeah…it's okay, Nell. You're safe."

"I—I thought you were one of them."

A note in his voice she hadn't heard before, he rapped, "Did they hurt you?"

"No—no, they just scared me. I'm all right."

She was shaking in reaction, like aspen leaves in the lightest of breezes, her fingers clutching at his shirt as though she'd never let go. Kyle took her in the circle of his arms, drawing her close, his hands rhythmically stroking her back. "I didn't mean to scare you," he murmured. "But I didn't want you screaming your head off so that the whole bunch of them came charging through the woods to the rescue."

"What are you doing here anyway?"

"I couldn't sleep. That's when I saw the lights on the beach. Figured I'd take a look and make sure you were okay."

With a little sigh, Nell collapsed against his chest. She muttered, "We've got to stop bumping into each other like this."

"You're right…you pack a punch, lady."

She slid her arms around him. The curve of his rib cage, the flat belly, the hardness of his breastbone, she remembered them all. "It was nice of you to think about me."

"Especially after you said you didn't want to see me again."

"So I did. Why couldn't you sleep?"

"Never you mind."

His cheek was resting on her hair, a state of affairs that she liked very much. She murmured, "You smell nice."

"So do you," Kyle said.

Against her face she could feel the roughness of his body hair at the neckline of his shirt; it seemed the most natural thing in the world to nuzzle at it with her lips. Warmth began to spread through her body, her shivering changing its tone so gradually she was scarcely aware of what was happening.

"Don't do that!" he choked.

Her head reared back. "What's wrong?"

Easing his hips away from hers, he said grimly, "Do I have to spell it out for you?"

"You mean you…" Nell flushed scarlet, stepped

backward, tripped over a tree root and sat down hard on the puffy folds of her sleeping bag. It failed to pad the root. "Ouch!" she said.

Kyle reached down and hauled her to her feet. "What in hell are you doing junketing through the woods with a sleeping bag?"

"I was going to find a dry spot and go back to sleep," Nell replied with as much dignity as she could muster. "You swear too much."

"There's something about you that brings out the worst in me. One aspect of which is swearing. I don't suppose it's a two-person sleeping bag?"

"It is not."

"Too bad. Because I'm not leaving you out in the woods alone while those party animals do their best to tear up the beach. You've got two choices. We'll go to the bungalow where I'm staying—you can have my bed and I'll bunk down in the living room on the chesterfield. Or else the two of us'll stay out here for the rest of the night."

It was cold in the woods, and her bottom was still smarting where it had connected with the root. "Let's go to the bed-and-breakfast," she said meekly. "As long as we won't disturb the owners."

"My God—no arguments?"

"Would they do any good?"

"No. Here, take my hand."

He led the way to the path on the ridge, and within minutes they were walking along the paved road, Kyle favoring his left leg. The beach party was still going full blast. "I hope they don't touch my tent," Nell said.

"If they do, they'll have me to reckon with."

She had never before allowed a man to protect her. She rather liked it. "How's your knee?" she asked.

"Fine."

Nell was light-headed with tiredness, the waning

moon was casting a silver sheen on the ocean, and Kyle
was still holding her hand even though he didn't really
need to. She said vigorously, "I was scared back there
in the woods, right?"

"So you should have been. You notice I haven't said
I told you so?"

"That's very noble of you. I was scared, I let you see
I was scared and I was happy to be rescued. So I don't
think it would hurt you one bit, Kyle Marshall, to tell
me that your knee's sore—sore as hell, as you no doubt
would say—and that perhaps we should walk a little
slower."

He stopped dead in the middle of the road. "Maybe
you came to Newfoundland because all the eligible men
in Europe got together and bought your airline ticket."

"How's your knee, Kyle?"

"I bet they even chased you onto the plane."

"Answer the question!"

"Hurts like hell," he said cheerfully. "But if we walk
any slower, I'll be tempted to kiss you again. You were
dynamite in the daytime. I hate to think what you'd be
like by moonlight."

"That's only sex," Nell said testily.

"Nothing wrong with sex."

How would she know? "One more thing," she said
with considerable determination. "*You* take the bed, *I*
take the chesterfield."

"Don't want to talk about sex, Nell?"

"Do shut up, Kyle!"

"*I'll* take the chesterfield. When the owners wake up
in the morning I think it would be better if they find me
in the living room rather than a woman they've never
seen before."

"Breakfast," she said wryly, "could be a most interesting meal…mmm, smell the roses."

Kyle had unlatched the gate in a neat white picket

fence that was overhung with a tangle of old-fashioned roses. He ushered her in the front door of the bungalow, where she bent and took off her hiking boots. The interior of the house was newly painted, sparklingly clean and decorated with starched lace doilies on every available surface; night-lights were plugged into sockets in the kitchen and hallway. Feeling a little guilty that she would be taking advantage of Kyle's sore knee, Nell tiptoed into the living room while he was still awkwardly untying his boots; she lay down flat on the chesterfield with her sleeping bag in a mound on her feet, gripping her haversack to her chest.

Kyle padded into the room. In a hoarse whisper, he ordered, "Nell, get up."

She had no idea a whisper could sound so adamant. "It's very bad for you to have your own way all the time."

He advanced on her. "Just because my knee is sore doesn't mean I'm totally incapacitated."

In the dim light, her eyes were dancing. "You'll have to remove me bodily. During which process I shall contrive to drop my water bottle on the floor as noisily as possible. You'd hate for the owners to discover you carrying me into your bedroom at four o'clock in the morning."

"How bored all those men in Europe must be without you," Kyle murmured. "You win. Sweet dreams and pleasant awakenings." He limped into the first room off the hall and closed the door softly behind him. He had made no attempt to kiss her good-night.

After pulling a rude face at the blank white-painted panels, Nell deposited her haversack on the carpet, arranged the cushions to suit her and snuggled into her sleeping bag. Within moments, she was asleep.

In her dreams, Kyle was waving a bouquet of bog laurel at her from his seat in Wendell's truck, and the eagle had stolen her water bottle. Nell buried her face in the stream to get a drink. But the stream was warm and rough and smelled rather peculiar— Her eyes flew open.

Her nose was being thoroughly licked by a very large dog with mournful brown eyes. "*Jasses*!" Nell exclaimed, and burrowed her face into her elbow. Whereupon the dog licked her ear.

"What does that mean?" Kyle asked with genuine interest.

Nell sat up, scrubbing her nose with her sleeve. "It means yuk, ugh, disgusting and gross."

"Good morning to you, too," Kyle said.

She scowled at him. "Pleasant awakenings—so that's what you meant."

"His name is Sherlock." The dog was sitting back on its heels. It was a bloodhound, lugubrious of face and drooping of jowl. "He's quite old, very deaf, and loves all the guests— Oh, good morning, Gladys. This is Nell. Remember I mentioned last night that she was camped by the beach? Well, the party got a little rowdy. So I brought her here."

"Them young fellas, they only go there once a month or so, but when they take over that beach they make more noise than the gulls on the first day of lobster season. How do you do, dear? I bet you're hungry. How about some nice pancakes and bacon?"

Gladys was fiftyish, with tight gray curls and matronly hips. "I hope we didn't disturb you," Nell said.

"Arthur and me, we'll sleep through the Second Coming." Gladys chuckled heartily at her own joke. "You make yourself right at home, dear. I'll go put the coffee on."

Kyle's hair was damp from the shower and he was clean shaven. Feeling very much at a disadvantage, Nell got to her feet. Her hair was tumbling to her shoulders and her clothes were crumpled from having slept in them. She said warily, "Where's the bathroom?"

"End of the hall." He thrust his hands deep in his pockets. "Those caribou have a lot to answer for."

"Just what do you mean by that?"

"Without them, we wouldn't have met."

Although the look on his face was inscrutable, his gist seemed entirely clear to Nell. He'd rather not have met her. Which, when she was suffering from an almost uncontrollable urge to kiss him good-morning, was a lousy way to begin the day. Nell said, "I have one unbreakable rule—no arguments before I have my first cup of coffee. Excuse me, please."

She picked up her haversack, edged past him and hurried down the hall toward the bathroom.

CHAPTER THREE

A SHOWER did wonders for Nell. Her haversack always contained her toilet articles. She'd borrowed Gladys's hair dryer and had just finished brushing out her long hair when Kyle tapped on the door. "Pancakes are ready."

She could braid it later. Nell opened the door. "Lead me to them," she said.

But Kyle's big body was blocking the hallway, and there was something in his face that stopped her in her tracks. He reached out one hand, letting his fingers slide the length of her hair, gathering a handful of it and lifting it to his cheek. As though he was paying homage to her, Nell felt, and knew, absurdly, that she wanted to cry.

He said huskily, "You're so beautiful. So alive. I..."

But as she waited, breathless, his mouth suddenly tightened. A flash of pain, so short-lived that she might have imagined it, banished the tenderness that had suffused his features, and with shocking violence he dropped her hair, wiping his palm down his jeans as though her touch had contaminated him. Turning on his heel, he grated, "Come on. Gladys is waiting for us."

Numbly, Nell followed him through the living room and into the kitchen, which smelled deliciously of hot coffee and bacon. She carried on a conversation with Gladys that apparently made sense, she avoided looking at Kyle and she drained her coffee mug in record time. During this process, anger slowly began to spread through her, like the heat of the coffee. How dare Kyle treat her as though she were a mechanical doll, something to be turned on and off with the flick of a switch!

34

But as she munched on apple pancakes drenched in syrup, she remembered the way pain had ripped away his gentleness and stole a glance at him through her lashes. If her past had its demons, so, too, did his; not for the first time she wondered how he had hurt his knee.

"Last night, Kyle said you were all the way from Holland, dear," Gladys said, passing her the butter. "Now what brought you to Caplin Bay? You can't even find it on some of the maps."

In the shower, Nell had had time to think. She didn't want to camp in Caplin Bay again tonight, even though she was sure the partygoers were all nursing horrendous hangovers and would go nowhere near the beach. Furthermore, her money was limited, and she'd spent the better part of two weeks putting off the meeting that was the real reason for her trip. She said with a modicum of truth, "Ever since I arrived in Newfoundland I've been hearing about the outports—the settlements that you can only reach by boat. I'd like to stay in one for a while. So today I plan to take the coastal boat to Mort Harbour."

Although she had rehearsed this sentence while she was rinsing her hair, somehow it didn't sound as convincing as she would have liked. However, Gladys apparently noticed nothing amiss. "Well now, that's nice, dear. You and Kyle can go together."

Nell's jaw dropped. "*You're* going to Mort Harbour, Kyle?"

"That's the plan," he said evenly.

"Why are you going?"

"To visit friends of a good friend of mine."

His reason sounded no more convincing than her own. Although she couldn't very well say that. "What time does the boat go?" she asked weakly.

"Four o'clock," Gladys said. "Want I should call Mary and make reservations for you, dear?"

Nell already knew that Mary Beattie owned the only guest house in Mort Harbour and she'd already decided she must stay there for a few days because it was the obvious way to get to know the people who lived in the outport. "All right," she said. "I'll start out there anyway. Thanks, Gladys."

Within minutes, Gladys was putting down the phone. "You're all set. Good thing we phoned. She only has two rooms and Kyle had reserved the other one."

Nell's eyes flew to his. "Aren't you staying with your friends?"

"No," he said.

Quit prying was what he was really saying. "You were right about those caribou," Nell announced.

"You told me you couldn't afford bed-and-breakfasts."

Because Nell was essentially a truthful woman, she tended to trip herself up when she did lie. "My financial state is really none of your business," she said loftily, and speared another pancake.

"We're never told what the princess says to St. George after he rescues her, are we?" Kyle said unpleasantly, and got up from the table. "Thank you, Gladys. I'll be back later to get my stuff."

He had disappeared by the time Nell finished eating. She went to the beach and collected her gear, then did a wash and hung it on Gladys's line. The wind billowed through it, ballooning her T-shirts as though they all contained women in the last stages of pregnancy. Like her grandmother all those years ago, Nell reflected, and went for a brisk hike along the shore. It took only the first five minutes for her to conclude she couldn't possibly plan a strategy for meeting her grandfather; she simply had to wait on events. The rest of the walk she spent trying not to think about anything but the white-caps on the water and the gulls wheeling and dipping on the wind. Worrying about her grandfather was a totally nonproductive pursuit. And, apparently, she would have met Kyle sooner or later anyway; Mort Harbour was definitely too small for a man like Kyle Marshall to remain anonymous.

Was the good friend he had mentioned a woman?

With vicious strength, she fired a rock into the tumbling waves. His past couldn't have been devoid of women. Women in the plural. Not one of whom was any of her business. If she'd been smart, she'd have come straight from St. John's to Mort Harbour, rather than allowing herself to be seduced by the beauties of the national park at Terra Nova. Then she wouldn't have met him.

She tramped another two miles along the rocky beach, ate a banana and a muffin for lunch, then hiked back to Gladys's. Her clothes were dry. She repacked her gear under Sherlock's reproachful brown eyes, left money for Gladys and headed for the wharf. Kyle was already there. She nodded at him distantly and marched up the gangplank to board the boat, a move that felt every bit as momentous as entering the huge jet in Amsterdam that had brought her across the Atlantic.

The coastal boat, stout and sturdy, rather like an overgrown tug, had a passenger lounge, a snack bar and a big shed for freight anchored on the deck. It was clearly a working boat; yet there was an air of sociability about it that Nell found very appealing. She propped her pack by the shed, watching as boxes of groceries and supplies were casually handed down from the dock and stacked in the shed with no system that she could discern. At about quarter past four, the gangplank was drawn up, the mooring lines were thrown on board and the captain blasted a signal as they pulled away from the dock. The strip of water widened.

Nell moved to the stern, staring mesmerized at the

wake. She was on the last lap of a journey that had
started the day she had read her grandmother's diary in
the attic of the old brick house that belonged to Nell's
mother and father, the house where Nell had grown up.
The diary, musty smelling, the ink faded, had described
at great length all the members of Anna's family, her
friends, the fears of war, the hunger and travails of the
occupation. But then had come the liberation, and the
diary had changed. There were no more close-written
pages dense with adjective and adverb. Instead, the entries were terse, with big gaps between them.

A Canadian regiment had been billeted for a weekend
in the village of Kleinmeer where Anna lived. Anna had
met one of the soldiers and instantly fallen in love with
him. His name was Conrad Gillis, and he was from a
little place called Mort Harbour in Newfoundland. De-
lirious with the joy of liberation and the pangs of love,
Anna had taken Conrad to the old barn on her uncle's
farm. There they'd made love several times. Anna's ac-
tual words had been cryptic: "We have been together in
the barn. The sun caught the dust in the air and danced
with it. I didn't tell him I love him." Then Conrad's
regiment had to leave and Anna discovered she was
pregnant.

"My *moeder* and my *vader* say I may keep the child
and live with them. I am lucky. My friend, Anneke, is
being forced to give up her baby…I have made inquiries.
Conrad is married. So there will be no marriage for me.
I have brought disgrace upon my family in the eyes of
the village. The only thing I am glad of is that I didn't
tell him I love him…Today my daughter, Gertruda, was
born." And there the entries had ended.

Gertruda was Nell's mother.

The spaces between these short sentences had seemed
to reverberate with all that had not been said. The village
was small. Gertruda would have grown up knowing she

was different, that somehow her very presence had brought shame upon the family. No wonder she had moved away from Kleinmeer as soon as she was old enough. No wonder she had embraced a rigorous respectability and the strictest of rules and had married a man twenty-seven years her senior in whom there was no spark of passion. No wonder she had warned Nell against the perils of sex.

The tragedy was that Gertruda had been dead two months before Nell had found the diary; so Nell could never tell her mother that now she understood her behavior. Understood and forgave. For Nell had suffered from the stultifying atmosphere of the old brick house: the lack of laughter, fun and play; the harsh rules that had set her apart from the other children; the sense of secrecy, of things kept from her that, nevertheless, affected her every move.

As far as she could remember, she had only met Anna once, and that was when she, Nell, had been very young, perhaps three or four. She had known she had a grandmother; she had also known, with a child's perceptiveness, that this grandmother was not to be discussed.

And now she was on her way to meet Anna's lover, Conrad Gillis. He, she could only assume, could have no idea that he had fathered a child in a foreign land or that he had a Dutch granddaughter. Her attempts to write a letter that would break this news to him before she arrived on his doorstep had all ended in the wastebasket—crumpled balls of paper that failed miserably to communicate what surely could only be said face-to-face.

So here she was on *Fortune II* on her way to Mort Harbour. She had made inquiries to ascertain that Conrad was still alive and living in the same place. And that was the extent of her knowledge. Except that she was scared to death.

From behind her, Kyle said, "You look as though you're trying to solve all the world's problems."

They had moved beyond the shelter of Caplin Bay into more open water; the boat was heaving on the swell. Balancing against the rail, Nell turned to face him. "Just my own," she said lightly. "How long will it take us to get there?"

"At least two hours—it's on the far shore of the peninsula. And what are your problems, Petronella Cornelia?"

"Whether or not I'll get seasick," she said dulcetly.

"Right," he replied wryly. "The wind's sou'west—it'll get rougher yet."

He was standing astride, his hair a dark tangle, his jacket flattened to his chest. "I bet you don't get seasick," Nell said.

"My dad was a fisherman—I was brought up around boats."

Unable to contain a strong curiosity to know more about Kyle, Nell asked, "Here in Newfoundland?"

"A little outport on the northern peninsula. In those days, the coastal boat came twice a year, and there were no roads." He grimaced. "It's all too easy to romanticize the outports, especially in these days of urban blight. But even though the fishing was good, my family was always dirt poor. Worked day and night and never got ahead."

Although his clothes were casual, they weren't cheap; she had instantly recognized the label on his rain jacket. "You don't look poor now," Nell ventured.

"I got out—as soon as I could. And I stayed away." He scowled at her. "Why am I telling you all this? I never talk about myself."

"Are you married?" Appalled by her wayward tongue, Nell added in a rush, "Scrap that question. It's nothing to me whether you're married or not."

The bow of *Fortune II* rose to meet the swell, and spray lashed her cheek, plastering her hair to her head. "We'd better move forward before we get soaked," Kyle said. He grabbed her arm, and together they lurched to the shelter of the bridge. Bracing himself with an arm above her head, he said, unsmiling, "No, I'm not married. Came close once, but it didn't work out. Is there a man in Europe waiting for you to come home?"

She shook her head. The wind was snapping the flag at the stern and flinging rough-edged curtains of spray against the shed, and perhaps it was this that made her blurt, "I don't want to go back to Holland. I want to stay here."

"In Newfoundland? Forget it, Nell. The economy's the pits."

Her need had nothing to do with the economy; somehow she had expected Kyle to understand that. Obscurely disappointed, she watched the spume streak backward from the caps of the waves.

"Holland's your home," he added reasonably. "That's where you belong."

"No, I don't! I don't care if I *ever* go back." She suddenly couldn't bear the closeness of his big body. Ducking beneath his arm, she lunged for the railing that was on the lee side of the boat and stared out over the wind-whipped water, knowing that her eyes were stinging with tears. Then she saw his hands grip the rail on either side of her so that she was encircled by him. Twisting around, she choked, "And don't you dare laugh at me!"

"I hate to see you cry," he said in an odd voice. "You're running away from a man, aren't you, Nell?"

"I don't let men close enough to me that I have to run away. It's this place...there's something about it. I feel as though I've come home, as though I've found whatever I was searching for without even knowing I needed it.''

The boat plunged into a trough. Nell staggered, banging her nose against the zipper on Kyle's jacket. He drew her closer, steadying her. ''Why don't you let men close to you?''

''Why haven't you ever married?'' she countered.

''We both have secrets. That's what you're really saying.''

''Doesn't everyone?'' she asked with a touch of bitterness. She had grown up in a household of secrets. Secrets that made her the woman she was.

''*I* sure have,'' Kyle said, and for a moment his irises turned the same color as the black and depthless ocean. Then, in an abrupt change of mood, he grinned down at her. ''I've got an idea—why don't we go up on the bridge? We can look at the charts and see where we're going.''

When he smiled at her like that, her very bones seemed to melt in her body. I'd probably jump off the bridge if he asked me to, she thought foolishly. ''Okay,'' she said.

''Newfoundland's a hell of a place to live, Nell,'' he said with sudden violence. ''Nine months of winter and three months of moose flies.''

She had the impression he was talking more to himself than to her. ''Where do *you* live?'' she said.

''At the moment, precisely nowhere. Come on, we're going to the bridge. First thing you know, I'll be spilling out my entire life story to those big blue eyes of yours.''

She said impetuously, ''I wish you would.''

''I'll tell you this much—I'm in no position right now to meet a woman, Nell.'' He let go of the railing. ''Now head for the ladder.''

''You're giving orders again.''

''You're damn right I am. Move it.''

"Only because I want to," she said haughtily, and began climbing the narrow stairs, clutching the wet railings as hard as she could.

The view was worth the climb. *Fortune II* was skirting the coastline, with its long range of rugged, tree-clad cliffs against which waterfalls spread their lacy white palms. Ragged, gray-edged clouds raced through the sky, daubing the hills with light and shadow. The captain pointed out deserted graveyards and abandoned settlements of indescribable loneliness, and in a manner that reminded Nell of Wendell, told her about the harrowing winters of the early settlers from Cornwall and Devon. Kyle drew her attention to nesting terns and the huge white gannets swooping close to the waves. And Nell fell in love even more deeply with a landscape as different from her homeland as it could be.

It's my grandfather's blood in me, she suddenly knew in a flash of insight. That's why I love this place. Of course it is. Why didn't I think of that before?

Somehow this realization seemed to conquer the fear that had been gnawing at her ever since she'd embarked on the coastal boat. But when, two hours later, she caught her first glimpse of the tiny outport of Mort Harbour through a gap in the cliffs, all her fears rushed back in full force. She glanced around to see where Kyle was, hoping he wasn't watching her.

He, too, was gazing at the little patch of houses whose presence seemed only to magnify the terrible fragility of human striving and the vastness of sea and land. The emotions on his face were as raw as the slash in the cliffs. Dread, Nell reflected, and a terrible reluctance, as if he'd rather be anywhere else than here. Emotions that were so akin to her own that she had to suppress the urge to rush over to him and offer him comfort.

He didn't look like a man who was simply visiting friends.

Secrets. He had as many as she.

She turned away, not wanting him to know she had seen feelings that were intensely private. The boat was entering the harbor, which was ringed by gaunt hills; like a womb it enclosed a long, low island in its calm inner waters. As they approached the government wharf, Nell saw little fish sheds on stilts at the cliff base, small square houses huddled together for solace, and brightly painted Cape Islanders rocking gently in the wake of the coastal boat's passing. What if her grandfather was away? Or ill? What if he wouldn't see her?

Her knuckles white with strain, she gripped the railing so tightly that her nails made tiny moons in the paint, and if she could have miraculously transported herself back to Middelhoven and her parents' old brick house with its tall windows and its yews in the front garden, she might well have done so. Then a hand dropped onto her sleeve, a man's hand with long, lean fingers and a dusting of dark hair over the taut bones. Kyle's hand. She wished him a thousand miles away.

"Nell, what's wrong?" he asked urgently.

She tried to pull her arm away. "Nothing."

"Don't give me that—something's up. You're not just a tourist checking out the quaint little Newfoundland outports. I know you're not."

"Stop it, Kyle!"

"You can trust me, you know," he said.

She couldn't tell anyone why she was here, not until she had spoken to Conrad. That much, at least, she owed her unknown grandfather. "Please—just leave me alone. You're imagining things."

"You're a terrible liar."

"Whereas you don't seem able to understand when you're not wanted," she declared, and saw an answering anger harden his features.

"That's the second time you've told me to get lost.

Guess I'm kind of a slow learner,'' he snarled. ''Why don't we just agree to have nothing to do with each other from now on? That, it seems to me, would be simpler all round.''

''I couldn't agree more,'' Nell retorted. Which was a lie if ever there was one. Until she'd met Kyle, she'd always considered herself a truthful person.

From directly above their heads, the boat's horn blasted its signal of arrival. Kyle flinched, his fingers digging into her arm as the shock ran through his body. His reaction seemed all out of proportion to Nell. She asked uncertainly, ''Are you okay?''

The engines had gone into reverse. Under cover of the noise, Kyle grated, ''You want it both ways, don't you? The sweet, womanly concern and the barefaced lies. I don't need either one, do you hear me?''

Because she couldn't possibly have told the truth about the purpose of her visit, Nell had done the opposite and lied. In the process, she'd lost something irretrievably precious: Kyle's trust. What more did she have to lose? ''You're not just visiting friends—I saw your face.''

''What I'm doing is my own goddamned business and not yours. From now on, stay out of my life, will you?''

''I don't care what you're doing!'' she cried, adding one more lie to the total. ''Just leave me alone!''

Unfortunately, the captain cut the engines on her last four words. Heads turned, and there was a titter of laughter from the other passengers.

''I will never again go anywhere near a caribou,'' Nell seethed, turned on her heel and seized her pack out of the shed. As the gangplank was lowered, she hung back, watching them unload the freight, steadfastly refusing to even look for Kyle. Not until the crowd had thinned on the wharf did she ask directions for Mary Beattie's house.

Long wooden boardwalks had been built across the rocks, linking the houses, the fish shacks and the general store. Nell tramped along, wondering where Conrad lived. She was only a few hundred feet from the square blue house that was Mary Beattie's when she saw Kyle emerge from the side door and start climbing the grassy slope behind the house. He had not, she was almost sure, seen her. At least she was spared making artificial conversation with him in front of her unknown landlady.

The blue house had bright pink trim, orange daylilies swarming around the side door, and scarlet geraniums lining a path outlined with white-painted rocks. Before she was even in the door, Nell felt her mouth lift in a smile; nothing could be further from the house where she had grown up. Mary Beattie was also a delight: young, pregnant and friendly. The only catch was that the two guest rooms shared a bathroom and were cut off from the kitchen and living room by a door that was kept firmly shut.

"You probably met Kyle on the boat," Mary said, leading Nell into a room that was a rampage of pink ruffles. "He's gone out to visit friends. But if you're ready, we could eat any time." Her face softened. "My Charlie's down at the wharf. But he'll be back for his dinner any minute now."

Charlie was burly and shy, leaving the talking to his wife. Nell tucked into the best haddock she'd ever eaten, along with peas from Mary's garden. "Not easy havin' a garden here," Mary said. "But Charlie does the heavy work, right, Charlie?"

Charlie nodded and took another potato. With a touch of wistfulness, Mary said, "I always grow tulips in the spring. I'd love to see the tulips where you come from, Nell."

So Nell found herself describing the bulb gardens in Keukenhof and the flower markets of Amsterdam, and by the time the meal was over she felt as though she'd made new friends. After supper she went for a walk, following Mary's directions to the trail that led behind Mort Harbour along the river that divided the settlement from the wilderness. The trail gradually descended to water level, where she saw kingfishers, and trout jumping in the still pools. A dozen or more boats were moored by a rocky beach. Maybe Charlie would take her up the river one day, she thought, and sat down on a rock to watch the sun sink behind the hills.

Purposely, she hadn't asked Mary about Conrad Gillis; she'd needed a respite after everything that had transpired between Kyle and herself. She'd ask tomorrow.

She wandered back to Mary's, trying her best to soak in the atmosphere of the place where, as far as she knew, her grandfather had always lived. She went to bed early, partly to avoid seeing Kyle, partly because she was as tired as if she'd been translating at a conference for eight hours without a break. She fell asleep right away.

When she woke, it was still dark. Her heart was pounding as if she'd been running, and her ears were straining at the blackness. Then she heard it again: a harsh, strangled cry that flooded her with atavistic fear. She flicked on the bedside light, scrambled out of bed, opened her door and was across the hall without even stopping to think. But even with that horrible sound echoing in her ears, she didn't quite have the courage to open Kyle's door. Instead, she tapped on the wooden panels. ''Kyle—are you all right?''

The door was flung open and she was confronted with an expanse of bare male chest and a fury so fierce that she took an instinctive step backward. Not just his chest was bare, she saw with a clarity that burned its way into her brain. He was wearing a pair of briefs and nothing else. Dark hair curled to his navel; his muscles were truly impressive. As impressive as his rage, she realized, and backed off another step.

"Go back to bed!" he rasped. "And for God's sake, leave me alone."

Calling on all her courage, Nell stood her ground. "I only wanted to help—I heard you cry out."

The light from her room sifted through the silk shift she was wearing; she had a weakness for silk and had chosen not to sleep in an old T-shirt just because she was backpacking. The shift covered her adequately enough from cleavage to thigh. But the pale gold light delineated the curve of her waist and hip and the jut of her breasts, as well as the sleek fall of her hair.

Kyle's eyes raked her from head to foot. "Yeah?" he said with dangerous softness. "I already told you to stay the hell out of my life. You'd better watch it, Nell. It's been a long time since I've had a woman. You keep on offering to help and I might decide to take you up on it. Your body's not bad. Not bad at all."

As his meaning slammed into her consciousness, she felt a flood of heat scorch her cheeks. "I wasn't throwing myself at you—I wasn't! That's the last thing I'd do."

"Really? After the way you kissed me by the grocery store? I have difficulty believing that. In fact, why don't you come in here? We're both wide awake and I've got a double bed—shame to let it go to waste."

Nell almost fell backward to her own doorway, clutching at the frame. "I hate you," she whispered. "I never want to see you again." Her fingers trembling with haste, she shut the door and shoved a wooden chair under the handle. Then she sat down hard on the bed, crossing her arms over her chest.

She felt dirty all over. Her mother was right. Sex was shameful. Men weren't to be trusted. How could Kyle, who had kissed her with such magical tenderness in the van, have spoken to her as if she were nothing but a cheap lay?

But there was more to it than that.

Neither her mother nor her father, so deadly respectable and so repressed, had ever allowed her to be close to them. Only the Bensons, the Canadian couple who had lived down the road and who had taught her English from the time she was four, had given her unstintingly of intimacy. That intimacy had flowed naturally from a marriage alive with passion and from myriad friendships that the child Nell had watched, wide-eyed and fascinated, from a safe distance. What Nell knew of love she had gleaned from Liana and Glen Benson. It was they who had encouraged her facility for languages and they who had urged her to leave the village for wider horizons.

Kyle was just one more person who didn't want intimacy. Or only an intimacy of the crudest sort, she thought with a shiver, remembering the way his eyes had traveled over her body and the ugly sneer in his voice.

Would Conrad Gillis allow her to become part of his life? Or would he, too, shut her out?

CHAPTER FOUR

BREAKFAST, so Mary had informed Nell, was between eight and nine. Nell lay rigid as a board listening to the hiss of Kyle's shower and the small sounds he made as he opened and closed doors. She then waited another half hour before getting up herself. So it was quarter to nine before she went into the kitchen, a kitchen blessedly empty of everyone but Mary. "Good morning," Nell said.

Mary shot a glance at Nell's shadowed lids. "Didn't sleep so good?" she asked. "Anytime I'm away from home, sleepin' is like tryin' to catch a fox in a trap. Oatmeal, Nell?"

With faint surprise, Nell realized she was hungry. She tucked into orange sections and thick creamy oatmeal, wondering how she could introduce Conrad's name into the conversation with any semblance of grace.

Then Mary said, "Kyle's moved out—gone to stay with Conrad and Elsie. So you'll have the place to yourself."

Nell choked on a mouthful of oatmeal and sputtered, "*Who*?"

"Kyle. The guy who stayed here last night. Big, good-lookin' fella—didn't you meet him?" She paused. "Are you okay?"

Nell cleared her throat. "I'm fine. What I meant was, who are Conrad and Elsie?"

"The Gillises," Mary replied, looking puzzled, but too polite to ask why Nell had reacted so strongly. "You passed their place if you walked upriver last evenin'."

"The white house by the waterfall?" Nell asked. She

had not only noticed the house, she had been struck both by the beauty of its setting and by its separation from the rest of Mort Harbour.

''That's it.''

Somehow Nell had pictured herself wandering along one of the boardwalks and casually opening a conversation with Conrad over the fence. A chance meeting that she wouldn't have to engineer. But the house by the waterfall had its own separate road. It wasn't a place where you could drop in.

Conrad and Elsie were the friends Kyle had come to visit. Kyle was the obvious person to introduce her to them. But Kyle had made it all too plain he never wanted to see her again. And she had told him she hated him.

Nell ate a slice of delicious homemade molasses bread and said more or less truthfully, ''Someone told me Conrad had served in Holland during the war. I thought I might ask him whereabouts he was. There were Canadians in the village where my mother grew up.''

''I don't know about that,'' Mary said dubiously. ''Seems like he's never talked about the war. Just wanted to forget it. He goes to the Armistice Day ceremony, but that's about it.''

So that avenue was closed to her. Swearwords in any one of five languages, Nell reflected, couldn't solve the dilemma of how she was going to meet Conrad, and meet him soon. Resolutely, she changed the subject. After breakfast, she insisted on packing her own sandwiches for lunch, promised to be home for supper by six and left the house.

She didn't know what either Conrad or Elsie looked like. So there was no use thinking she might bump into them; she wouldn't know them if she did. Nor could she very well hang around the road to their house and hope to see Kyle. He'd undoubtedly turn his back on her. Or drag her into the bushes, she imagined with a little shiver.

What was she to do?

She hoisted on her haversack, climbed the hill behind Mary's and looked around her. For the third day in a row, the sun was shining: a rarity in Newfoundland. The rocks and islands surrounding the harbor were frilled with white lace and threaded by dazzlingly white gulls; the grass underfoot was a rich, damp green, like plush velvet. My grandfather lives here, Nell thought, and part of me has always lived here. I know the place. It's in my bones.

She'd go down by the river, she decided. At least then she'd know she was close to Conrad.

The river trail passed above the house by the waterfall. She sat down on a rock and rested her chin on her hands. The vegetable garden was the biggest she'd yet seen, and the most sheltered. A white-haired woman in a housedress was bent over weeding. Was that Elsie, Conrad's wife? There was a very good chance that Elsie would hate Nell. For Nell was, after all, the tangible evidence of Conrad's infidelity.

Then, with a jolt of her heart, Nell saw Kyle come out of the back door. His long-limbed body and crop of dark hair were achingly familiar to her. He, too, was in her bones just as this place was.

And explain that, Nell Vandermeer.

From her perch, she watched him chat with Elsie, then vanish into the shed beside the house. When he emerged, he was carrying a fishing rod and a tackle bag. His limp barely noticeable, he walked partway up Percy's road, then cut up through the woods toward the river trail. Toward her.

For a crazy moment, she contemplated staying where she was. Take me fishing with you, Kyle, and then introduce me to your friends...is that what she'd say?

He'd laugh in her face. In sudden panic, she ducked behind some alders and went higher into the woods until she was screened from sight of the trail. Crouched low, she heard him pass; his tackle bag rattled with every step.

Without having made a conscious decision, Nell waited a few minutes, then followed him along the trail, sticking to the soft ground wherever possible, all her senses alert. When she peered around the curve to the rocky beach, she saw that he was already backing one of the dories out of its mooring, the motor purring.

In an ideal world, she reflected with a painful twist of her lips, she would be with him, heading upriver between tree-furred cliffs and scree-covered slopes, where the ravens swooped like fragments of night. As it was, Nell sat down on a boulder and began to think very hard. Kyle had to come back this way. This was her chance to meet Conrad.

When Kyle returned, she could be swimming in the pool nearest to Conrad's house. She'd stage some kind of accident so that Kyle would have to stop. So that he'd have to take her to Conrad's house. That's what she'd do.

Her conscience, always overly scrupulous, sat up straight. You're using him, it announced. Deceiving him shamelessly. He deserves better than that.

I have to meet Conrad.

And break Elsie's heart?

What else am I to do? Go back to Holland and pretend I never had a grandfather?

Leave well enough alone, her conscience said trenchantly. You've seen where Conrad lives. That's more than enough. Go home before you do irreparable damage to people who have never harmed you.

He did make love to my grandmother. Are you forgetting that?

Fifty years ago, Nell. Let bygones be bygones.

Did everyone's conscience speak in clichés? Nell
wondered gloomily. All she wanted to do was talk to
Conrad. Elsie wouldn't have to know who she was.

Good luck, her conscience sneered.

Oh, do be quiet, Nell grumbled silently.

Kyle's boat was out of sight now, hidden by a sheer
black cliff that looked as insurmountable as her difficulties. She wandered farther down the trail, absently
admiring the purple irises and the fluffy white meadow
rue that grew along the banks. Swallows were darting
low over the river, and delicate blue harebells sprouted
between the rocks. As the water burbled peacefully to
itself, her spirits gradually calmed. Her plan was the best
she could come up with. She couldn't go back to Holland without meeting Conrad. She wouldn't be able to
live with herself if she was that much of a coward.

She found a couple of flat rocks at the very edge of
the river, where the breeze kept the flies away, took out
a paperback she had bought in St. John's and began to
read. She ate her lunch, then chatted with two young
boys who were also going fishing. Then Nell started
back along the path. She had to pick her spot and re-
hearse her plan so there wouldn't be any hitches.

She spotted a deep pool that was out of sight of
Conrad's house, although only a few hundred feet away
from it; the pool was clearly visible from the river trail.
Nell climbed over the rocks, checking out the dark
brown water. The day was hot enough that a swim was
genuinely tempting, the only catch being the weeds that
waved lazily in the current. Nell didn't like waterweeds;
they were slimy and always made her think of eels. But
they gave her the perfect excuse why she'd slip and hurt
herself just as Kyle appeared at the far bend in the trail.

She'd pretend she'd hurt her ankle. That way, he'd

have to take her to Conrad's, not all the way back to
Mary's. And the rest would be up to her.

The pool was almost enclosed by rocks, rather like
the harbor itself. She walked out on the farthest ones,
from which vantage point she would be able to see
Kyle's boat returning. She hoped he wouldn't be long.
She didn't want to be late for dinner.

As though her fortunes had changed for the better,
barely fifteen minutes passed before Kyle's green dory
chugged around the bend, then disappeared as it headed
for the beach. Nell had already changed into her trim,
dark blue swimsuit and fastened her hair in a knot on
top of her head. She slipped into the water, gasped at
how cold it was and swam away from the rocks, all the
time keeping a careful eye on the trail.

Ten minutes later, she saw Kyle round the corner. He
was wearing rubber boots, jeans and a blindingly white
T-shirt. Her heart gave an uncomfortable lurch in her
breast. She turned her back on him and splashed around
vigorously, hoping to get his attention. Carefully guess-
ing how long it would take him to come level with her,
she then swam toward the weedy rocks, braced her feet
and began to haul herself out of the water.

Her heel slipped on the weeds. She grabbed for the
nearest rock. But it, too, was underwater and slimy to
the touch. Then a long furl of grass, cold and slippery,
brushed her leg, lazily coiling itself around her thigh.
With a whimper of panic, she twisted to escape it. Her
knee connected with the sharp edge of a boulder with
bruising force; her yelp of pain was entirely genuine.
She overbalanced and fell backward, her mouth agape
with surprise, for this had not been part of the plan.
Water gurgled down her throat and dragged at her hair.
As she flailed her way back into the light, her thigh
scraped the length of a rock that was as rough as sand-

paper. She gave another startled yelp and struggled to find a purchase among the weeds.

"Here—grab my hand!"

The plan had succeeded, Nell thought wildly, and seized Kyle's wrist as if it was a lifeline. Her hip bumped against a rock. He was kneeling as he lifted her, his forearms like thick bands of steel, although she did hear him grunt with effort as he swung her clear of the water. She pushed with her feet against a dry rock, trying to take some of her own weight, and fell into his arms in a way that couldn't have been more convincing had she rehearsed it.

Sputtering from water that seemed to have gone up her nose as well as down her throat, she managed to gasp, "Thanks."

Kyle said grimly, "There's a very basic rule—never swim alone. Remember that in the future, will you, Nell?"

Her ankle wasn't hurt. But her knee and her thigh were stinging abominably. Serves me right for being so deceitful, Nell scolded herself muzzily, and clung to him, the breeze chilling her body so that goose bumps sprang up on her flesh. Her head was butted under his chin; the heat of his chest only made her shiver the harder.

His arms tightened convulsively. "It's a damned good thing I came along when I did."

Feeling heartily ashamed of herself because, of course, the timing had been no accident, Nell said, "You're swearing again."

"My knee's half killing me, Nell—I've got to move." Then his voice changed. "For Pete's sake, you're bleeding. What have you done to yourself?"

"It was the rocks." She looked down, and her shudder was in no way feigned. Blood was trailing down her thigh, and her knee boasted an ugly graze. "I scraped against them when I was trying to get out of the water."

"You need a bodyguard," he said.

The words burst from her lips before she could stop them. "I wasn't trying to seduce you in the middle of the night at Mary's."

"If I try to pick you up with my knee bent under me, I'll be permanently crippled. Stand up, Nell. Then I'll do my macho bit and carry you to Conrad's. That scrape needs cleaning."

She pulled back from him. "Did you hear what I said?"

"I was in a foul mood last night."

"Next time you're in a foul mood, don't take it out on me!"

"No, ma'am," he said meekly.

She looked at him through wet lashes. His arm was still hard around her ribs, and his face was close enough that she could have traced his lips with her fingertip. She said, "You told me the very first day we met that my eyes reminded you of those little flowers. Do you know what your eyes are like? That moment at dusk when the sky's the darkest of blues, but not quite black. I lived in Amsterdam for a while and I hated not being able to see the night sky properly because of all the lights."

Sparks blazed in his eyes, like stars in the night sky. He said roughly, "Right now I want to make love to you so badly I can taste it. But that's not part of the plan, Nell. Stand up, and we'll go to Conrad's."

Nell, whose plan it was to go to Conrad's, could think of nothing to say. She knew she was blushing. It should have been from shame at her deception; but it wasn't. It was from sheer wonderment that Kyle found her desirable. She stood up, wincing from the pain in her leg.

Kyle slung her haversack and his tackle bag across his back, handed her the fishing rod and said gravely,

"Don't drop it. Elsie gave it to Conrad for his seventy-fifth birthday, and he makes no bones about the fact that he doesn't lend it to just anyone." Then he swung her up into his embrace.

Nell looped one arm around his neck. "I'm too heavy—you'll hurt your knee."

"It's not far."

She could see how the muscles along the crest of his shoulder had tautened to hold her; desire could be mutual, she thought. "You're supposed to tell me I'm the merest sylph and as light as a feather."

Laughter shook Kyle's chest. "But it wouldn't be true." His belt buckle was jammed into her hip. His rubber boots scuffed the trail. For an instant out of time, Nell was visited again by one of those moments of pure happiness. Kyle said huskily, "Keep looking at me like that, and we'll be heading for the bushes."

"Too many mosquitoes," Nell responded lightly. "Not to mention blackflies and moose flies. Passion and moose flies don't seem like a very good combination to me. Are Conrad and Elsie the friends you came to see?"

"Yes, they are, and I'd be willing to wager Conrad's fishing rod that I could make you forget all about moose flies," Kyle said, taking the left-hand fork that was Conrad's driveway.

"But Conrad would never speak to you if you lost."

"I wouldn't lose." He stopped for a minute, bent his head and found her mouth, his tongue flicking against her lips. In sheer surprise, Nell opened to him, heat spreading all the way to her belly as his kiss deepened. When he finally raised his head, her eyes were dazed and her lips a soft, vulnerable curve.

"No," she whispered, "I don't think you would lose."

A gravelly old voice said, "Now then, young lady, you be careful of that fishing rod."

Nell jumped and Kyle turned in his tracks. "Hi, Conrad," Kyle said. "Meet Nell."

Nell's deep blue eyes were still suffused with passion, and her cheeks were a delicate wash of pink. The old man standing in the driveway furrowed his brow, his mouth tightening. Staring at her as though he'd never seen a woman before, he muttered belligerently, "Who are you?"

He was a tall man, and although his muscles had wasted with age, Nell could see that he once must have been a force to reckon with. His hair was as white as the feathers of a gull, and his eyes were a deep blue. Very like her own, she realized, and felt panic close her throat.

Kyle said easily, "Nell's visiting Newfoundland—she was staying at Mary's last night."

Conrad took the fishing rod from her nerveless fingers and snorted, "Cat got your tongue? What parts d'you hail from?"

It was the moment of choice, Nell knew. She could remain anonymous or she could throw the first of her cards on the table. She swallowed a lump in her throat that felt like a rock and wished she were clad in more than a swimsuit. "Holland," she replied, "I'm from Holland. A little village called Middelhoven. But my people came from Kleinmeer." Then she watched as the color drained from Conrad's mottled cheeks.

Kyle said, "Conrad, what's the matter? You don't—"

But Conrad interrupted him, his bushy white brows drawn together in the fiercest of scowls. "Not all of us welcome strangers to these shores."

Nell raised her chin, looking, had she but known it, even more like the ardent and impetuous young woman her grandmother had once been. "Not even when others welcomed you to theirs?" she countered.

Unceremoniously, Kyle lowered her to the ground.

"What the hell's going on? She's hurt her leg, Conrad. I need to clean it before it gets infected—that's why she's here. It didn't occur to me you wouldn't want me to bring her here."

"Then you're not very smart," Conrad said, his ferocious old eyes impaling Nell as she stood, temporarily mute, in the circle of Kyle's arm, the slender lines of her figure dappled by the shadows of the trees. "You two can do what you like. Tell Elsie I'll be in the shed." Wielding the fishing rod as though it were a bayonet, he tramped across the gravel toward the red-roofed shed and did not once look back.

She should have written, Nell thought numbly. She should have warned him that she was coming. She could have addressed the envelope solely to him so that Elsie need not have read the letter. He might have a temper like an aging rooster, but he was still an elderly man whom she should have treated with more consideration. Terrified that by some chance Kyle might guess the truth, she said falteringly, "I—I thought all Newfoundlanders were friendly."

"He can be a cantankerous old guy, but I wouldn't have expected him to be openly rude like that." Kyle frowned. "It was almost as though you reminded him of something."

She couldn't bear Kyle even to entertain that possibility. Because, deep within her, Nell knew that all her hopes had been crushed in that one brief conversation. Conrad, she was almost sure, had remembered his long-ago infidelity and had guessed that she had some connection with it; and in a few rough words he had repudiated her.

With what she hoped was artistic flair, she limped across the driveway toward the house, flinching as the stones cut into her heels. "I'm cold," she said. "And I'm supposed to be at Mary's by six for dinner."

"I'll drive you," Kyle said absently, still gazing toward the shed. "Conrad's got an all-terrain vehicle."

Conrad would probably be delighted if she drove off the cliff, Nell supposed, then Kyle tucked his hand under her elbow.

"Leg hurting?" he asked.

His sympathy almost undid her. But she couldn't cry. Not now, when she was about to meet Conrad's wife. She nodded and followed him into a homey kitchen, with crisp white curtains and a profusion of African violets whose velvety blooms ranged from white to the deepest purple. An elderly woman was peeling potatoes in the sink. She wiped her hands on her apron and smiled at Nell—smiled with her whole face, holding nothing back. "Well, now, a visitor. But you've hurt your leg, dearie. How did that happen?"

That Conrad's wife should be so different from Conrad seemed another cruel blow; this time Nell couldn't repress the tears. She sank into the nearest chair. "I was s-swimming in the river."

"Kyle will look after you. You look cold as a sparrow in winter, dear. Let me make you a nice cup of tea. And here, wrap this shawl round you." As Kyle left the room, Elsie took a crocheted afghan from the rocking chair that stood by the woodstove and draped it over Nell's shoulders.

"But I'm muddy from the river," Nell protested.

"I can always wash it." Elsie patted her arm. "I'll get a towel for your hair, too."

The afghan smelled of lavender. I have to go away from here and never come back, Nell resolved. Because Elsie is the kindest person I've ever met, and I wouldn't hurt her for the world.

Elsie passed her a fluffy white towel and gave her another smile. It was a sweet smile; but Elsie's hazel eyes, Nell rather rapidly decided, wouldn't miss a trick.

Elsie, too, was white-haired, although her luxuriant bun made Nell think of a sweep of snow rather than predatory gulls. She was a small woman, still slim, her house-dress sprinkled with pink and red roses, her apron a long blue coverall. "My name's Elsie," she said, busying herself with the kettle. "And what would yours be?"

"Nell. I'm staying with Mary Beattie."

"Are you now? She's due in three months, I believe. The Lord never blessed Conrad and me with children, but I'm always happy when the young ones round here raise a family."

Conrad fathered a child, Nell couldn't help thinking. My mother. Hurry up, Kyle. I've got to get out of here.

"I don't blame you for going swimming," Elsie added. "The weather's been that warm the past few days, I haven't wanted to be cooking at all. There you are, Kyle. You'll have tea, too, won't you? And I bet both of you'd like cookies with your tea—oatmeal cookies, my grandmother's recipe. She came out from Devon and never went back. Fell in love with the place and with my grandfather. That's the way it goes, isn't it, dearie?"

Kyle was crouched by Nell's chair, his dark head brushing her arm. Not always, Nell thought. Not for me. Because I'm not in love with Kyle. It's Newfoundland I'm in love with.

His hands exquisitely gentle, Kyle bathed the graze with strong-smelling disinfectant, picking out flecks of mica with a pair of tweezers he'd taken from a worn leather bag. Elsie put flowered teacups on the table beside them and said, "There's nothing like having a doctor in the house, is there?"

"A doctor?" Nell repeated blankly.

"Finest one on the island, I'd say. If only he'd stay put here in Newfoundland—where his home is."

"We've already been through that, Elsie," Kyle said

in a voice that brooked no argument, then smeared the wound on Nell's knee with antibiotic ointment.

"The reason beach rocks are smooth is because the sea wears away at them," Elsie responded imperturbably. "Sugar, Nell?"

The tea was strong and hot, distracting Nell from the feel of Kyle's hands on her bruised and scraped thigh, and from her new knowledge that he was a doctor. If his parents had been dirt-poor, it must have been a struggle for him to go to medical school. Were his parents still alive? And why had she herself never asked him what he did? Perhaps, she realized, because every bit of information she gleaned about him seemed to bring him closer to her. "The cookies are wonderful," she said, and smiled at Elsie.

Kyle stood up. "I'll want to check your knee tomorrow," he said impersonally, and crossed the room to wash his hands at the sink.

"You must come for dinner tomorrow, dear," Elsie said. "I love to have company."

"Oh, no, I can't possibly do that," Nell said in a panic. "I'm going back to Caplin Bay tomorrow."

Kyle grabbed the towel hanging by the sink and said nastily, "How? Are you planning to swim? After half drowning yourself at the river's edge?"

She glared at him. "I'll take the boat."

Elsie said placidly, "It doesn't come back until tomorrow afternoon. Then it leaves again on Wednesday. And I've got a better idea. We're having a bunch of people here Wednesday evening to play a little music and some of the old songs. You must come, Nell."

"I really can't, Elsie. I have to get the boat on Wednesday and go—"

"I won't take no for an answer, dear," Elsie said. "It'll be a real Newfoundland mug-up, and you mustn't miss it. Only thing better is if you could be here over Christmas. We still do mumming in Mort Harbour.''

"Mumming?" Nell asked.

"People get dressed up in costumes and masks and go from house to house. You have to guess who they are, and sometimes it's downright impossible. You'd enjoy it." Briskly, she poured more tea in Nell's cup. "But Wednesday night will be a lot of fun and I'll look forward to seeing you again."

Nell was beginning to feel a bit like a beach rock herself, tumbled in tides that were paying not the slightest attention to her. Perhaps, she thought with a flash of humor, this was how Elsie dealt with Conrad. "It's very kind of you," she prevaricated, and inwardly knew she wouldn't come. She'd stay away from Elsie and Conrad all day tomorrow, and on Wednesday she'd get the boat. Mary would know the schedule.

"That's settled, then," Elsie said, beaming. "Now tell me about yourself. Where you're from, for starters."

"I'm from Holland."

"Are you now?" Elsie's face clouded. "Conrad was in Holland in the war. He never likes to talk about those years. Not even to me."

Could that be why Conrad had spoken to her so harshly? Nell wondered with a flicker of hope. Perhaps his reaction had had nothing to do with Anna, but only with horrible memories of an endless war. Perhaps she herself had been too quick to jump to conclusions. Feeling exhaustion seep through her limbs, she drained her cup and said, "Will you excuse me if I get changed? Mary's expecting me for dinner soon."

Elsie ushered her into a little guest bedroom upstairs, decorated charmingly in blue and white. Like Delft china, Nell mused, stripping off her damp suit and wriggling into her shorts and T-shirt. Her hair was a mess, and she looked pale and tired. But what did it matter?

After Wednesday, she wouldn't be seeing Kyle or Elsie again. She'd be heading back to St. John's as fast as she could.

A dark cloud of misery had settled itself somewhere in the vicinity of Nell's heart. She would have liked to have flung herself down on the pristine white bedspread and cried her eyes out. You can't, she told herself fiercely. You've got to get out of here without Elsie so much as suspecting you came for a reason. That's what you've got to do.

She stuck a smile on her face and walked back down to the kitchen. "Ready?" Kyle asked.

"Thank you so much, Elsie," Nell said. "You've been very kind to me."

"Wednesday, don't forget now. Come around five for dinner. Mary and Charlie are invited, so you can walk over with them."

Nell could think of nothing to say to this. "Bye," she said softly, and on impulse dropped a kiss on Elsie's withered cheek. Elsie, like the afghan, smelled sweetly of lavender. As quickly as she could, ignoring the pain in her knee because it couldn't compare with the pain in her heart, Nell walked outside.

Kyle said abruptly, "Why are you in such an all-fired hurry to catch the boat?"

"That's surely my affair," Nell said crisply, and hobbled toward the vehicle parked by the shed.

He stationed himself in front of her. "Sunday you're in a hurry to get here and Monday you can't wait to leave? It doesn't compute, Nell."

"I don't want to talk about it!"

"It's something to do with Conrad and Elsie, isn't it?"

Spacing each word, she repeated emphatically, "I do not want to talk about it. Have you got that? And if you won't take me back to Mary's right now, I'll darn well walk.''

"He'll take you," Conrad said. "Catch." And he tossed the key in Kyle's direction.

As Kyle deftly caught it, Conrad looked straight at Nell. Go away, his very bearing said to her. Go away and don't come back.

She refused to drop her gaze. I'm going, she retorted inwardly. But not because of you. Because of Elsie. She cleared her throat and said with assumed calm, "Goodbye, Conrad."

He said nothing, standing as stiffly as a soldier on guard as Nell perched herself on the back seat of the ATV and Kyle started the engine. As the four fat tires took purchase in the gravel, the ATV surged up the hill. At any other time, Nell would have enjoyed bouncing over the rocks and sailing along the boardwalks. But not today. Today she would have given her soul to have seen *Fortune II* anchored at the wharf, ready to take her as far away from here as she could go.

Kyle pulled up below Mary's and turned off the engine. The silence rang in Nell's ears. He slid to the ground and said flatly, "You look exhausted. I wish you'd tell me what's wrong, Nell."

"I can't," she said raggedly, and knew her words spoke the truth. "I can't tell anyone—it's not just you."

"Some secrets are better for sharing."

"Not this one."

"So there *is* something going on...."

"Kyle," Nell said with the last of her energy, "are you prepared to tell me what woke you in the night at Mary's? What your nightmare was about?"

His jaw tightened. "Intimacy—that's what neither one of us is ready for."

"I guess so." How could she be, when on Wednesday she'd be gone? All she'd have left would be memories of Kyle's midnight blue eyes, his explosive temperament and his rare laughter. With an unhappy smile, she said, "You're right. I am exhausted. Goodbye, Kyle. Thanks for driving me home."

"I'll come by tomorrow afternoon and take a look at your knee." He dropped a kiss on her cheek and stepped back. "You liked Elsie, didn't you?"

"Yes," Nell said, avoiding his gaze, "I liked Elsie." She picked up her haversack and plodded up the path between the scarlet geraniums. I liked Elsie so much that I'm leaving here before I do her any harm. And I'm leaving you, as well, Kyle Marshall, before I do anything silly like make love to you.

My grandmother made love with a stranger years ago and paid for it dearly. I won't do the same.

Because if I have secrets, so do you.

CHAPTER FIVE

By TUESDAY midday, Nell was in possession of the information she needed. *Fortune II* arrived in port that afternoon and left the next morning at ten. And she would be on it.

It rained heavily all day Tuesday. She had spent a quiet morning around the house with Mary; and her decision, difficult though it was, gave her a measure of calm. All she had to do was hold on to that calm until after Kyle's visit this afternoon. Then she would leave Mort Harbour the next day, leave Newfoundland as soon as she could and go back to Europe and her job as a translator. She'd forget about a land that had called to her soul, a grandfather who had repudiated her, and a man who had awoken her to the wonders of desire. There would be other places as beautiful. Of course there would be. And—who knows?—perhaps there would be another man whose touch would bring her body to life.

All these tidy conclusions flew straight out of the door as Kyle walked in it. He was wearing yellow oilskins, rain dripping from the hood and spiking his dark lashes. A lock of hair clung to his forehead. He grinned at her. "Conrad's as cross as a bear, and Elsie's making enough pies and cakes to stock a bakery. Offer me a cup of tea, Nell, for heaven's sake."

"How about a shot of rum?" she returned wryly.

"Now you're talking."

She took his jacket and hung it over the hook, watching as he shucked off his rubber boots and the baggy yellow trousers. His worn jeans clung to his thighs and his narrow hips; his sweatshirt bared his strong wrists and the hollow at the base of his throat. "Hold still," she said, and brushed his hair back from his forehead.

His skin was cold. But the look in his eyes was not.

She was also wearing slim-fitting jeans, with a ribbed blue turtleneck that outlined her small, firm breasts. Her hair was looped back with a blue ribbon that Mary had given her. Kyle said softly, "Come here."

It never occurred to Nell to tell him he was giving her orders again, any more than it occurred to her to argue. She walked into his embrace as if she was going home, then lifted her face for his kiss. It was a kiss that lasted a very long time; neither of them noticed Mary walk into the kitchen, smile to herself and tiptoe out again.

Finally, against her mouth, Kyle murmured, "I think this is called intimacy, Nell."

Her breasts were molded to his chest, her flesh ached to be rid of her clothes, and her carefully constructed calmness had drowned in a desire as wild as the sea. She confessed, for once wanting no secrets, "I have never in my whole life responded to a man the way I do to you."

She was glowing like a candle, lit from within, and her gaze was as clear and honest as the small blue flowers he used to pluck as a boy. Kyle said huskily, "You make me forget that there's anything in the world but your beauty and your warmth. Which, for me, is new, too."

Then he kissed her again, and words dropped away. He drew her full against the length of his body so that with a fierce pang of passion she felt the hardness of his erection. Then as his other hand found the rise of her breast, caressing it to its tip, Nell for the first time understood how Anna could have thrown away all caution and restraint in the desperate search for fulfillment that a man's body could grant.

When Kyle eventually released her, Nell could barely

stand up. She whispered, "I need a doctor—I'm about to faint and fall in a heap at your feet."

"I'm not sure medical ethics would approve of what I'd prescribe."

Wide-eyed, she asked, "And what would your prescription be?"

"A week in bed. With the doctor."

Nell replied pertly, "Would that bring about a cure?"

"It might. Or it might just make the malady worse. What do you think, Petronella Cornelia?"

"I can't think. That's one of the symptoms."

He brushed her lips with lingering pleasure, his dark eyes laughing at her. "Where's Mary?"

Nell had completely forgotten about Mary. "She's probably hiding out in the bathroom. It's called tact."

"Maybe I should take a look at your knee," Kyle said.

"How dull," Nell teased. "How worthy."

He laughed out loud. "The alternative is for us to make love on the porch floor. Upon which my oilskins have dripped rather copiously."

"Afraid of a little water, Kyle?"

"Afraid of you," he answered with sudden, unconstrained honesty. "Afraid if we do make love, I won't be able to walk away from you."

Shaken, Nell said, "That's exactly how I feel."

"Then I suggest we cool it, rescue Mary from the bathroom and see if all that disinfectant did its job yesterday."

"I—I'll go and change into my shorts," Nell mumbled. "I'll be right back." As she crossed the kitchen, she called, "Mary—Kyle's here." Then she disappeared into her bedroom.

The woman in the mirror was a stranger to her. A beautiful stranger, she observed with an odd humility. A stranger who definitely would have made love to Kyle on the porch floor, water or no water.

And then what? Would she have been able to get on the boat the next day and sail away from Mort Harbour? Which is what, for Elsie's sake, she had to do. She had no choice.

Nell fumbled in her drawer for her shorts, changed into them and, when she glanced in the mirror on her way out the door, saw an altogether different woman, one who now looked careworn and unhappy, all her glow and sparkle gone.

It seemed an appropriate occasion for a profusion of swearwords. Pulling a face at herself, Nell walked back to the kitchen in time to hear Mary say shyly, "Nell tells me you're a doctor, Kyle. D'you mind checkin' me over? The nearest doctor's in St. Swithin's, and Charlie and me can't get over there that often."

Kyle hesitated, his big body very still. "It's years since I've practiced in Canada, Mary—I've been overseas."

"A pregnant woman's the same the world over," Mary persisted.

Nell could almost see his inner struggle, one whose sources she could only guess at. He raked his fingers through his hair and said, "My bag's just by the door. I'll be right back." He conducted a swift but thorough examination, pronounced mother and child in the best of health, then turned to Nell's knee. "Clean as a whistle," he pronounced with considerable satisfaction. "I'd stay out of the river for a couple more days, though, Nell."

"All right," she agreed, and with a sinking of her heart she knew she was deceiving him again.

He stayed for tea and chocolate squares, then said cheerfully as he left, "See you both tomorrow night. Elsie's looking forward to seeing you again, Nell—she really took to you."

Nell winced inwardly. "It was mutual," she replied with careful truth. "Bye, Kyle."

She closed the door on his back and was glad Mary was in the kitchen so she, Nell, wouldn't be tempted to watch his tall figure disappear down the path. Glad, too, that there had been no opportunity for another of those devastating kisses.

She had to leave Mort Harbour. Because of Elsie.

She should never have come.

When she climbed out of bed on Wednesday morning, Nell's resolve was unchanged. While her knee was sore, her emotions felt as though they'd been slowly and agonizingly scraped across a thousand rocks. In the pale light of dawn, it seemed obvious that Conrad's reaction in the driveway had been far too strong to have emerged from the mere fact that she was Dutch and had consequently aroused in him memories of war. No, it had been more personal than that. She had reminded him of Anna. She had brought back memories of a past he had long ago buried; nor was he going to allow it to be disinterred.

That was why he wanted to be rid of her and—for his wife's sake—that was why she was going.

By quarter to ten, Nell was standing on the deck of *Fortune II*, tucked under the bridge on the side of the boat away from the wharf. Mary, fortunately, had gone to the grocery store to buy vegetables for the casserole she was planning to make for Elsie's party. Nell had written Mary a note that was a careful mix of truth and untruth, had propped it up on the kitchen table and hurried to the wharf. Her backpack was resting in the scuppers. With every nerve in her body, she strained to hear the blast on the horn that would signal their departure.

The water was smooth as oil; fog hung offshore, blotting out the cliffs, smothering the islands. Nell knew that leaving Mort Harbour was the right thing to do. She couldn't live with herself if she caused Elsie to doubt a lifelong marriage. She also knew it hurt abominably.

Now that she had failed, she realized how deeply she had cherished the dream of finding a new family in this rugged land. One that would welcome her as her own never had. Added to that pain was a deeper and less easily explicable pain. Kyle. Nell gazed into the murky water. How, in a few short days and with a few magical kisses, had he reached a place within her that no other man had ever approached? A place she hadn't even known existed.

How would she ever forget him?

Boots rasped on the metal steps behind her. In sudden intuition, she turned her head, and as though her thoughts had called him up, she met Kyle's stormy dark eyes. He was wearing the same sweatshirt as yesterday and the same yellow oilskin jacket. He looked formidably angry.

He said in a clipped voice, "I figured this is where I'd find you."

All Nell's pain transformed itself into a matching anger. "I should have locked myself in the washroom. Not even you would come after me there."

"Don't bet on it." He took her by the sleeve. "Sneaking away without even saying goodbye. I never thought you were a coward."

Anger peaked to rage. "It's precisely because I'm not a coward that I'm leaving!"

"Oh, you're not leaving," he said grimly.

She struggled for restraint. "This is a public place and I'm not going to have a shouting match with you. Goodbye, Kyle. There, I've said it. Are you satisfied?"

"You left a note for Mary. But you didn't have the guts to leave one for me."

She had hurt him, she realized with a sharp pain in her breast. "I didn't leave you a note, no."

"I don't rate one," he snarled.

"I didn't know what to say—that's why!"

"Why don't you try telling the truth for once? That'd be a novelty."

The men who had been loading the freight had slowed in their task. A couple of passengers had come out of the lounge and were listening in a fascinated silence. But what did she care? After today she'd never see them again. Or Kyle. Nell blazed, "Okay! How about this for truth? You and I haven't made love yet. So you can still walk away from me, Kyle Marshall. None of that intimacy you're so scared of. None of your secrets exposed to the light of day. Did it ever occur to you that that's why I'm leaving?"

He said softly, yet with an intensity that pierced through her rage, "Is it, Nell? Is that why you're leaving?"

Her shoulders sagged. "No. No, it's not."

"Then why?"

"I can't tell you, Kyle," she admitted in a low voice. "I'm not being difficult, I'm not playing mind games, and it's not because I don't know what I'm doing. I do know. But I simply cannot tell you about it. You've got to believe me."

She watched as he took a deep breath; the pulse was pounding at the base of his throat. I want you, she thought. I want you and I have to leave. He said roughly, "When you look at me like that—do you have any idea what it does to me?"

With a faint smile, she said, "I can guess."

He was standing so close to her that as he took another deep breath she felt it fan her cheek. He jammed his fists into the pockets of his jeans and asked, "Do you have a plane ticket to Amsterdam in the next five days?"

"No." Her ticket was open.

"You already told me there isn't a man waiting for you somewhere in Europe."

She replied warily, "That's right."

"Do you hate fiddle tunes and folk songs?"

"No. But that's not—"

He rested a finger on her lips; it felt cold against her skin. "Let's leave you and me out of this for now. Elsie's counting on your being there tonight, Nell. I haven't known Elsie and Conrad for very long, but I'll tell you something. You touched Elsie in a way that was somehow unique. You wouldn't believe the questions she's asked about you, most of which I can't answer because I don't know the answers. After Conrad had gone to bed last night she told me what a sorrow it's been to her that she couldn't have children. Maybe you somehow fill that gap, or maybe she mothers all strangers who cross her threshold. I don't know. I do know that if you leave like this, without going to her party and without saying goodbye, she'll be very hurt. Is that what you want?"

Nonplussed, Nell gazed up at him. Then the horn gave its deep, one-note roar from the bridge. She closed her eyes, feeling confused and besieged. Conrad, unbeknownst to Elsie, had a granddaughter of his own blood. Would that bring Elsie more happiness than unhappiness? Could the pleasure of having a grandchild outweigh the sure knowledge of infidelity?

How could she, Nell, possibly know the answer to her own questions?

"You takin' the boat, Kyle?" the captain shouted down. "We're pullin' up the gangplank."

Nell looked up. The captain and the purser were grinning down at them, and the crowd around the door of the lounge had increased. In true anguish, she cried, "I don't know what to do! I had it all figured out until you came along."

Kyle bent and hefted her pack onto his back. "You're getting off this boat and you're going to Elsie's party tonight. That's what you're doing. Move it. We're holding up Transport Canada."

One of the crew members was untying the gangplank; metal screeched on metal as he hauled it toward the vessel. Nell bit her lip. "You're giving me orders again."

"You're damn right I am."

"And you're swearing."

Kyle kissed Nell hard on her open mouth. Then, with a wicked smile, he strode across the deck and hefted her pack up to one of the men standing on the wharf, a burly man in a skintight shirt, with arms like a wrestler's. He crossed the deck again, this time picking Nell up. "If I keep hanging around you, I'm going to have to take up weight lifting," he said, and crossed the deck once again. "Think you can handle her, Pete?" he called up.

"Sure can," Pete said, flexing his muscles.

The sea monsters tattooed on his arms wriggled and writhed. Nell scrunched her eyes shut, recalling the coils of the waterweeds, and felt herself being transferred from Kyle's arms to Pete's, lifted through the air, then put onto the ground with surprising gentleness. She opened her eyes and said with a politeness her mother would have applauded, "Thank you, Pete."

"No sweat."

Pete stretched a hamlike fist down to Kyle, who clambered over the edge of the wharf, put his arms around Nell and said, the same wicked gleam in his eye, "Let's give them something to remember us by."

"Kyle," she chided, "I think we already have."

"The finishing touch," he said, "the climax—although not the kind I'm interested in," and kissed her with a thoroughness and an evident pleasure that her mother would not have applauded.

The people on the deck applauded, however, as did

the small crowd on the wharf. The captain blew the horn again, and *Fortune II* churned the water into a hiss of bubbles as it edged clear of the wooden pilings.

Too late now, Nell thought. I'm staying.

The crowd began to disperse. "See you at Elsie's," Pete said, mounted a bright purple ATV and drove away.

Kyle said calmly, "Let's take your pack back to Mary's and hope we get there before she reads your note."

Nell's emotions were in such a turmoil she wasn't sure if she wanted to laugh or cry. Or both at once. Panic, delight, foreboding, anger. They swirled around her like the winds of the sea. "You can carry the pack," she said, and heard the quiver in her voice.

"Nell, it'll be all right," Kyle said soberly. "Whatever's going on—it'll turn out just fine."

She said with enormous dignity, "You go on ahead and I shall walk three steps behind you, as befits a woman who's just allowed a man to talk her into something she had no intentions of doing."

"How about walking beside me instead?"

Exasperated, she cried, "Hurry up, Kyle. I don't want Mary finding that note any more than you do."

But Kyle walked slowly enough that she did indeed end up beside him. And what that meant, Nell had no idea.

She bent to untie her hiking boots in the back porch when she got to Mary's. So Kyle went into the kitchen ahead of her. She heard him say, "Oh…Mary, you're back."

"What's all this about Nell? She's gone?"

Nell shucked off her second boot and stepped into the kitchen. Mary was holding the single sheet of paper over which Nell had so painstakingly labored. "I didn't go," Nell said.

Mary gaped at her. "What's goin' on?"

Nell said weakly, "I changed my mind."

"I changed it for her," Kyle said.

"Don't sound so self-satisfied," Nell snapped. "You may live to regret that move."

He was openly laughing at her. "Regret it? How could I, Nell? I'm sure it's very good for me not to have a clue in hell what's going on behind that pretty face of yours. I do tend to be into control, as you may have noticed."

"You're not the only one who doesn't have a clue," Mary announced. "I'm glad you stayed, though, Nell. Charlie and me were lookin' forward to goin' with you tonight. You don't want to miss a get-together at Elsie's—they're special."

"Conrad, I gather, brews a spruce beer that could make a lighthouse fall on its face," Kyle remarked.

"It can make Charlie get up and dance," Mary said. "And that's somethin', let me tell you. Put it alongside Elsie's partridgeberry pie and Samson McFarlane's fiddlin' and you've got yourself a party."

Nell could fight Kyle. But she couldn't fight the combined forces of Kyle, Mary, spruce beer and partridgeberry pie. "I don't have any fancy clothes," she said in a resigned voice.

"I've got a dress'd be perfect on you." Mary patted her own girth. "I sure won't be wearin' it. You go on home now, Kyle. Us women've got things to do."

And Kyle, to Nell's amusement, winked at her and went.

He was no sooner out the door than Mary said sternly, "Now that's a good man, unless pregnancy's addled my brain. Seems like he's taken with you."

"He's taken with getting his own way."

"Then he might just have met his match, right? Whatever's the reason, I'm real glad you changed your mind,

Nell. Now—you want to help me mix up a batch of bread and make the casserole?''

Touched by Mary's honesty, Nell said, ''Thanks, Mary. Sure, I'd love to.''

So instead of being carried away across the bay, farther and farther from Kyle and Conrad, Nell spent the day cooking and talking to Mary. Mary told the story of how she met Charlie, whose excessive shyness had almost thwarted their romance, and then told some of the old stories about the hardships in the settlement in its early days. Nell found herself describing her childhood, its happy times as well as its loneliness, trying to paint a picture of growing up in a small village in Holland. The kitchen filled with the delicious scent of baking bread; the casserole was adorned with parsley and Parmesan and stored in the refrigerator.

Mary, Nell was beginning to realize, had considerable organizational talents. When the bread was done, Nell's hair was the next project. Mary arranged it in a loose knot on the back of Nell's head, with tendrils falling around her face, tendrils that looked casual and took some concentrated effort to achieve. Mary then shared the contents of her makeup kit and brought out the dress, a very pretty dress with cap sleeves and a scooped neckline, its mauve rayon fabric sprinkled with spring flowers, its full skirt swirling around Nell's legs.

''I knew it'd fit you,'' Mary said. ''Hides the bandage on your knee, too.''

More than that, it made Nell feel feminine and flirtatious. She pirouetted to admire herself in the long mirror in Mary's bedroom, delighted when Mary's strappy sandals fit her, too.

''Wore them on my weddin' day,'' Mary revealed.

''But won't you want them tonight?''

''Haven't worn heels since I got pregnant. Don't want to risk anythin' happenin' to this baby.'' She chuckled

as she gave Nell the once-over. "Kyle won't know what
hit him. You go do your nails and put on some makeup
while I get ready. Then Charlie can have the bathroom.
Oh, and put the casserole in the oven, would you? We'll
take it heated up."

Nell took her time with her nails and makeup and was
more than pleased with the results. If she was going to
confront Conrad again—because he couldn't very well
skulk in the shed all evening if the party was at his
house—she was going to do it in style. As for Kyle, it
wouldn't hurt him to see her in something other than
jeans or shorts.

She rather hoped he wouldn't know what hit him. It
would serve him right for lifting her off the deck of
Fortune II as though she were nothing but a sack of
potatoes.

Why had he wanted her to stay? Only to save Elsie's
feelings? Or were his own feelings tangled in there
somewhere?

If they were, he'd probably be the last one to admit
it, she reflected caustically. When he'd spoken to her
about control, he hadn't told her anything she didn't already know. Carefully, she applied a smooth coating of
soft pink lipstick. Her earrings were the final touch—
small gold seagulls whose widespread wings gently
bumped against her neck. They'd been her one extrav-
agance since she'd come to Newfoundland; she'd found
them in a boutique in St. John's.

She was ready. She busied herself slicing Mary's
bread and arranging it in a woven basket, and half an
hour later, she, Mary and Charlie were walking into
Elsie and Conrad's kitchen.

CHAPTER SIX

THE kitchen was crowded with people whose mood was clearly convivial and who were nearly all strangers to Nell. Then Elsie saw her and hurried to give her a hug. "I heard you almost left today on the boat," she said. "We'd have been real disappointed, wouldn't we, Conrad?"

Conrad, standing behind Elsie, didn't hug Nell. He gave a noncommittal grunt and made rather a business of relieving Charlie of the casserole.

But Elsie wasn't through. "They said it was Kyle who stopped you. I made a special point of thanking him." Her eyes twinkled. "Although I don't suppose the reason he stopped you was anything to do with me or the party, dear...oh, there you are, Kyle."

Kyle looked magnificent in dark linen trousers and a loose-fitting silk shirt. He also looked suitably stunned by her appearance, Nell thought, and said demurely, "Good evening, Kyle."

He declared hoarsely, "I didn't think you could be any more beautiful than you were that first evening we met. You take my breath away, Nell."

A gratified sigh went around the room. Abandoning any pretense at respectability, Nell said, "Whereas you look extremely sexy."

"Oh," he returned, "you look sexy, too. That goes without saying."

"Feel free to say it anytime you like."

"Since you wouldn't be standing here listening to how sexy you are if it hadn't been for me, don't you think I deserve a hug?"

From the corner of her eye, Nell had sighted someone who wasn't a complete stranger. "Pete helped," she teased, "so he deserves one, as well."

"No," Kyle contradicted, "it's me you'll hug, Petronella Cornelia." And suited actions to the words.

His arms drew her the length of his body; his kiss transferred pink lipstick from her mouth to his and left her weak at the knees. But she wasn't going to tell him that. Nell took a tissue from her pocket, scrubbed at his lips and murmured, "I'll have to ask for a refund. It was supposed to be kissproof as well as waterproof."

"Modern technology can only do so much." Kyle grinned. "Want some of Conrad's spruce beer?"

She batted her extralong lashes. "I'm always open to new experiences."

"Glad to hear it," he said, turned around and started threading his way toward an impromptu bar on the far wall.

Everyone started talking at once, and Nell let out a pent-up breath. Her mother and father would disown her for that little scene. But Anna, her passionate and wayward grandmother, might not. As though that thought were the cue, she found herself looking straight into Conrad's baleful blue eyes. She glared right back and said softly, for his ears alone, "I did my best to leave. It's Kyle you should be angry with, not me."

She might just as well have saved her breath. "We'll have a little talk later," Conrad muttered. "Once the music's started."

"I'll look forward to it," she lied, and gave Kyle a brilliant smile as he edged toward her, a glass of foaming dark liquid held over his head. The spruce beer was potent stuff. Nearly as potent as Kyle, Nell decided. "You realize we've fed the gossips of Mort Harbour for the next week," she said amicably. "Do you always chase your women so publicly?"

"It's been so long, I can't remember."

"You expect me to believe that? An utterly gorgeous hunk like you?"

He nearly choked on his beer. "Do you always flatter your men so outrageously?"

"I'm only trying to tell the truth. As you requested." Her eyes sparkled. "Although I can't say I'm telling the whole truth—that really would embarrass you. And me, too, probably."

"The next boat doesn't leave until Sunday. Do you think between now and then there's the slightest chance I'll figure out what's going on inside that extraordinarily decorative head of yours?"

They appeared to have joined a lineup for the food table. Nell laughed. "It took Mary the better part of the afternoon to decorate my head. Enjoy it. I'll be back to normal tomorrow."

"You give the word 'normal' a whole new dimension," Kyle remarked dryly. "Are we supposed to dance after eating all this?"

The long table was laden with casseroles, salads, relishes and breads. "You Newfoundlanders are tough— look on it as a challenge," Nell said, and picked up a plate.

When she reached the end of the table, her plate was piled high. She headed for the parlor, where chairs were set up all around the room, and sat down next to Pete, whose tattoos were concealed by an orange cotton shirt and whose wife was a sweet-faced woman called Ruth. Kyle sat down on Nell's other side, and they talked about everything from the windmills in Holland to the virtually nonexistent fishing off the Grand Banks.

Then Ruth excused herself to check her dessert in the oven. Pete looked down at his empty plate. "That tasted like more." He put down his glass and stood. "Looks to me like you're glad you stayed," he said to Nell.

The truth was getting to be a habit. "I wouldn't have missed this for the world," she said.

"Ellie Jane Groves was on the boat. So the story'll be all over Newfoundland by now. Ellie Jane has relatives in places you've never heard of."

"My fifteen minutes of fame," Nell quipped wryly.

But Pete was following his own train of thought. "When I started datin' Ruth, she took some convincin'. Had to show her I wasn't as tough as I look. Takes all kinds, you know," he finished cryptically, and strolled toward the kitchen.

"Advice to the lovelorn?" Kyle drawled.

More sharply than she intended, Nell said, "That lets me out." Looking anywhere but at Kyle, she noticed for the first time a cluster of photographs on the little table behind Pete's chair. She got up, as curious to learn more about Conrad and Elsie as she was anxious to escape Kyle. Then, from among the images, one leaped out at her: two men smiling at the camera, both wearing khaki uniforms and blue berets. One of the men was Kyle, a younger and more carefree Kyle. The other man had carrot red hair. Nell asked, "Is that your friend, the one you mentioned?"

Kyle scowled. "I haven't been in the parlor before tonight. I hadn't realized Elsie had kept that photo. Yeah, it's Danny."

"That's the UN peacekeeping uniform. Where was the photo taken?"

"Cambodia. Do you want something more to eat?"

"I'm saving up for dessert. What were you doing in Cambodia?"

"We were overseeing an election."

"Is that where you hurt your leg?"

"No."

Every muscle in Kyle's body seemed to have tightened. She said gently, "Tell me how you got hurt."

"Nell, I hate talking about it."

She gave him a long, thoughtful look. "If it wasn't for you, I wouldn't be here right now. I don't think you tossed me off the deck of *Fortune II* just so we could talk about cod fishing."

He answered rapidly, "I got hurt in Bosnia. Danny and I and seven others were hostages for several days when the safe area we were in suddenly turned unsafe. I caught a sniper's bullet."

"And Danny?" Nell prompted.

"Danny's transferred out of there now. But he wanted me to come and see Conrad and Elsie—they more or less brought him up because his mother and father drowned when he was young. I was at a loose end, so I came."

"On the coastal boat you looked as though you were dreading getting here. Is that because you knew you'd have to talk to Elsie and Conrad about what happened?"

"Great diagnosis," Kyle drawled sarcastically. "You should be the doctor, not me."

Nell didn't rise to the bait. "Were you on a medical team there?"

He nodded. "Let's go find dessert," he said restlessly. "I really don't like to talk about it."

"I can understand why—I've watched the news and read the papers," she said. "Did you volunteer?"

"Yeah...but don't make me into some kind of saint. I'd been on a six-month course just before that, and Angela—the woman I was engaged to—contrived to have an affair with a buddy of mine while I was gone. So I broke the engagement and signed up to go on UN missions." His smile was crooked. "Nothing very heroic about that."

Angela. Nell disliked the name instantly and the woman even more. Kyle must have been very much in love with her to have asked her to marry him. How could she have been unfaithful to him? And with a friend of his?

"You look homicidal," Kyle remarked.

She glanced up and saw that the lines of his face had relaxed considerably. "How could she have done that?" Nell retorted violently. "She must have broken your heart."

"There were a few days—and nights—when I thought she had. But now that I look back, it was my pride that took the beating, not my heart. My buddy, in the long run, did me a favor."

"But you must have loved her if you proposed to her."

"I thought I did. I was young, Nell, younger than you, and nearly all my friends were getting married. Besides, Angela was very beautiful." His smile was rueful. "I was also too young to figure out how she got to be so skillful in bed."

Nell's scowl, if anything, deepened; she didn't want to hear about Angela's skills in or out of the bedroom. But especially in. "Is she the reason you've never married?"

"I've been overseas ever since. Cambodia, Haiti, the Middle East and then Bosnia. Not exactly the way to foster a long-term relationship."

"I think she did a dreadful thing!"

"She saved me from making a bad marriage, and if I didn't know you better I'd say you were jealous."

Her eyes flew to meet his, and hot color scorched her cheeks. She *was* jealous, horribly, scaldingly, jealous. "Let's go and get some of Elsie's partridgeberry pie," Nell said crossly. "Before there's none left."

"This morning, you were boarding the boat without bothering to say goodbye to me, and now you look as though you'd like to murder my former fiancée. How in hell am I supposed to understand you, will you tell me that?''

"I don't know—I don't understand myself! Pie, Kyle.''

"Pie, or large quantities of spruce beer,'' he rejoined. "Lead on.''

As she walked back into the kitchen, stopping to chat with Charlie for a moment, Nell wished passionately that she could be alone for a few minutes. That brief conversation in the parlor had given her the key to understanding much of Kyle's behavior. She was convinced of it. But she needed to be alone to put all the pieces together. Later, she resolved. I'll slip outside once we've eaten.

The partridgeberry pie, served warm with thick cream, would have defeated the willpower of even the most dedicated dieter. Nell also had some of Ruth's blueberry grunt and a slab of rich chocolate cake. She said to Kyle, who had slathered his cake with ice cream and chocolate sauce and was determinedly sticking to her side, "I'm going to have to dance. The alternative is to fall asleep.''

"Samson's tuning up his fiddle—hear him?'' Kyle's dark blue eyes were smiling at her without artifice, and the silk shirt subtly emphasized the lean strength of his body.

"I'm really glad you got back from Bosnia safely,'' Nell blurted, then stood up, clutching her plate. "I'm going to help with the dishes for a while.''

As he stood up, too, it was as though they were alone in the room. He wound one of the loose tendrils of her hair around his finger and with his other hand stroked the line of her cheek. "Do you think we were meant to meet like this?'' he said. "That there was a reason I sighted those caribou and tripped over you on the barrens?''

Her lashes flickered. "It's not why I came to Newfoundland."

"Nor me. Although I'll tell you something. The day you tell me why you came to Newfoundland is the day I'll figure I'm starting to make progress." In sudden impatience, he dropped his hands. "Hell, I don't know what gets into me when I'm near you. I'm not into chasing women, and right now is the worst of times."

"Why?" Nell whispered.

"Oh, I'll probably be telling you that any day now," he said irritably. "Believe it or not, I had a reputation in the forces for being closemouthed."

"I believe it," she said, and quirked her brow. "But you hadn't met me then, had you?"

"Dishes," Kyle said with a lazy grin, pushing her in the direction of the kitchen with a hand at her elbow. "Women's work."

She bent to pick up two other plates, added them to her own and passed him the whole pile. "I just changed my mind," she said sweetly. "You can take these into the kitchen. I'm going upstairs to repair my lipstick."

He casually interposed his body between her and the rest of the room. Balancing the plates against his chest, he bent forward and kissed her with sensuous leisure. "Thought I should take advantage of your lipstickless state," he murmured, running his tongue along her lower lip.

Sex, according to Nell's mother, was a shameful and furtive business; nothing like the sunburst of pleasure that Kyle's kisses aroused, or the fierce urge to prolong that pleasure, or the delicious melting of Nell's limbs. Why should one be warned against something so natural and so seemingly inevitable? Why should it be turned into something ugly? "Good luck in the kitchen," Nell muttered, then hurried toward the narrow flight of stairs.

When she came back down, there was no sign of

Kyle. It was her opportunity to slip outside. She edged past the groups of men who were smoking and drinking beer on the big deck that overlooked the river and wandered farther down the driveway as it curved away from the house, sticking to the grass verge to protect Mary's sandals from the rocks. The waterfall's steady roar filled her ears. The sun was dipping toward the hills; the trees, the water, the darting swallows were all touched with gold. Gold and magic, Nell mused. With a sigh of contentment, she leaned against the trunk of a maple and let her body feel the ache of desire that Kyle could arouse by a look, a touch, a kiss.

Desire had never had anything to do with her mother's dark warnings. No, they had been oriented around shame. Passion—of any kind—had been anathema to her mother. The other gardens along the road in Middelhoven had boasted rosebushes and richly scented honeysuckle and rainbowed zinnias. Her mother's garden had consisted of four dark yew bushes and a square of grass from which any dandelions were ruthlessly uprooted as soon as they bloomed.

It would have been natural, and perhaps excusable, for Nell to have rebelled against her mother once she was on her own, and indulged in a series of affairs. But something had always held her back. The ingrained pervasiveness of Gertruda's voice? Or had it been an instinctual knowledge that—like her grandmother—she needed a man to touch her soul as well as her body?

Maybe, Nell reflected, her mother had been wrong all those years. It wasn't sex that was the issue. It was deeper and more complex than that. It was whether you were willing to risk your emotions. To ride the tide of passion and thereby make yourself vulnerable. Gertruda, she was almost sure, had never taken that risk with her husband and certainly hadn't with her daughter.

"You and I need to have a little talk."

Nell jumped and turned her head. Conrad was standing only a few feet away from her; the sound of the waterfall had covered his footsteps. She straightened, her heart pounding, and said with assumed calm, "Yes, we do."

"Why don't you start? Seeing as how you're the one who turned up on my doorstep out of the blue. What are you here for?"

He was facing the sun, which gilded his hair like the helmet of an ancient warrior. For this was war, Nell knew. Open war. She said clearly, "I came to find my grandfather. Whose name is Conrad Gillis."

Conrad's lips thinned. "Yeah? Tell me more."

"My grandmother's name was Anna Joost. She lived in the village of Kleinmeer. She met you in the last days of the war, when the Canadians liberated Holland. After you left, she had an illegitimate child—my mother, Gertruda."

"The father could have been anyone," Conrad said harshly.

"No. She left a diary, you see. She names you. You and Mort Harbour. And she described the way the hay dust drifted in the sunbeams that came through the windows of the barn."

Something flickered across Conrad's face. But he was not so easily defeated. "That was a long time ago. Why've you waited this long?"

"Because I didn't know about it. My mother died four months ago. Two months later, I found Anna's diary among some old papers in the attic. And I read it. That's why I'm here."

His face as unyielding as the granite outcrops in the river, he demanded, "What do you want out of this?"

"What are you willing to give?" Nell said, and knew it was a crucial question.

He sneered, "Not much money here—you can see that for yourself."

Cut to the quick, Nell was tricked into revealing the truth. "I don't want your money—that's the last thing I want! I'd hoped to find acceptance. Even love."

Conrad gave a short laugh that had not a trace of humor in it. "What about the rest of your family?"

"I'm the only one left. Anna died eighteen years ago. I traced the burial records. My father died eight years later. And I'm an only child." With real bitterness, she added, "No more grandchildren will be turning up to haunt you, Conrad. Unless you seduced other Dutch women while you were away."

He said heavily, "You're nothing but trouble to me."

Why should the words hurt so, when his every action since she had first seen him had told her as much? "This morning I tried to leave!"

"Then try harder."

She forgot about pride, her hand outstretched in a silent plea. "You don't want me? Not at all?"

"I want you gone."

From a long way away, Nell felt her thumb brush her thigh as her hand fell to her side. She took a step toward him, the roar of the river and the tumult of her own feelings somehow indistinguishable. "Did it never occur to you that you might have fathered a child?"

"I never gave it another thought."

So much for Anna's love. So much for Anna's pain and her lifelong shame, a shame that Nell had, indirectly, inherited. She said icily, "I don't like you very much."

"I don't give a damn! After today, you stay away from my house and my wife. And on Sunday get on that boat and don't ever come back."

Rage rushed in to replace the desolation in Nell's heart. "That would suit you just fine, wouldn't it?" she stormed. "No responsibility for your actions, no voices

from the past calling you to accountability. Let me tell
you something, Conrad Gillis. I've suffered because of
you. My mother left her home in Kleinmeer as soon as
she was old enough—she was a bastard, a disgrace to
the community. She moved fifty miles away and brought
me up so rigidly that I'm scared to death to go to bed
with a man and I'm—''

''Kyle'll fix that,'' Conrad said crudely.

Nell's shoulders sagged. There was no reaching him,
she thought in despair. ''Kyle is the reason I'm here
tonight,'' she said in a low voice. ''If you want to get
rid of me, you'll have to get rid of him, too. Which
might be a little more difficult.''

Conrad took a step closer. ''You just make sure you're
on that boat on Sunday. I'll look after the rest.''

''But you're my grandfather!'' she cried with the last
of her courage. ''Don't you even *care*?''

As though her words had been a trigger, he said with
raw honesty, ''I'll tell you what I care about. I care about
Elsie. My wife. And it'd take more than you to make
me change that.''

''You think I don't understand that? Why else did I
tell all those lies to Kyle and Mary and get on the boat
this morning?''

''I've had enough of this,'' Conrad spat. ''Go away
and stay away. You're not wanted here.''

Chewing on her lip in a frantic effort to keep tears at
bay, Nell watched him stride up the driveway and disappear around the corner. She couldn't afford to cry. She
had to go back to the party and dance and laugh and
have a good time. All under Kyle's all-too-shrewd gaze
and Elsie's concerned one.

How could Anna have fallen in love with someone as
hateful as Conrad? And if he loved Elsie that much, why
had he been unfaithful to her?

What does it matter, Nell? It's all in the past and better forgotten. That's what Conrad was trying to get across.

She had the beginnings of a headache. If the spruce beer didn't taste so awful, she'd go back to the house and get royally drunk, she thought with a desperate attempt at humor. Then she'd have a legitimate excuse for a headache.

Legitimate. Bad choice of words, Nell.

She tried to relax the tension in her shoulders. She tried to tell herself she'd lost something she'd never had, so why should it matter to her? But nothing made any difference. And then, from the deck, drifted the sound of a single violin playing a slow lament, the notes sliding over melancholy and despair and human folly until Nell felt her own tears slide down her cheeks.

She cried quietly, from a pain and loneliness that felt too deep for sobbing and wailing. The sun, with symbolic aptitude, sank behind the hills. The river gurgled and splashed its own secrets, offering her no comfort. The violin drew out the last long note until it slipped into the dusk and disappeared.

With a wild energy, the fiddler began a reel, its beat tugging at Nell relentlessly, daring her to resist it. Carefully, she dabbed at her cheeks with the skirt of Mary's dress. She'd go in the back door. That way she'd avoid the deck and the kitchen, and she could creep up the back stairs that she'd noticed earlier when she'd been upstairs. In the bathroom, she could repair her makeup before she had to face anyone. Like Kyle.

She traced her steps up the driveway, then took a little trail through the trees before she reached the deck. She walked past raspberry canes and a big rhubarb patch without seeing anyone or being seen. Well done, Nell, she told herself, and reached for the door handle.

Kyle came around the far side of the house.

CHAPTER SEVEN

"THERE you are, Nell," Kyle said easily. "I've been looking all over for you. I wanted to..." His voice changed. "Nell? Have you been crying?"

"No! Well, yes. But—"

His voice changed again, to something more dangerous. "What's wrong? Did someone upset you?"

She said raggedly, "Kyle, please don't ask me to explain."

He stepped closer, tracing a tear mark on her cheek with one finger. "I hate to see you cry. What in hell's teeth's going on around here?"

"It's not my secret to tell," she said desperately. "And I won't lie to you." The expression on his face was such a mixture of fierce protectiveness and a deep frustration that she should keep him so distant that Nell's mind made an all-important leap. Her next words came straight from the heart, cutting through her own misery, because her need to erase that frustration and allow Kyle to be close to her was stronger than her unhappiness. "Would you do something for me?" she asked, and with an inner trembling she prayed that he wouldn't reject her. "Would you just hold on to me for a while?"

Wordlessly, Kyle drew her toward him. Nell leaned into his chest and closed her eyes. His heart was beating against her cheek, heavy, slow strokes that were immensely comforting. The warmth of his skin seeped through his thin silk shirt; and that, too, was comforting.

The terrible loneliness that had made her cry by the river faded away like the light fading from the sky. She said quietly, "You know what? You make me feel safe. Safer than I've ever felt in my life."

"I do?"

"Oh, yes."

A tremor rippled through his body. In a voice so low she could barely hear him, he said, "There was a young woman in a little town near Visoko. She'd been raped. Before we could get to her, they shot her. I'll never forget how helpless I felt. How angry, and how goddamn helpless."

Nell put her arms around his waist, burrowing her face into his chest. What could she say to that? There were no words, none that were not either trite or facile. So she simply held on to him with all her strength, trying with her body to express the inexpressible; and she knew with total certainty that whatever was between her and Kyle had just shifted to a new level of intimacy from which there would be no easy retreat. Not for her. And maybe not for him, either.

The dying breeze rustled the leaves. A bird cheeped from the shrubbery. Eventually, Kyle slackened his hold, his eyes searching her face. "You look better," he said, "but your mascara doesn't."

She wasn't going to let him away with that. "Thank you, Kyle," she said gravely. "For holding me, and for telling me about the woman."

"This place is a long way from Bosnia."

"Memories go everywhere you go. Memories and nightmares."

He said huskily, "I'm glad you felt safe."

His very profession was dedicated to the saving of life; it must have torn him apart to be a helpless bystander to suffering and death. She said, "I know there's no comparison, no possible comparison between here and there. Nevertheless, although you couldn't help her, you have helped me. I want you to know that."

"Then it's my turn to say thanks."

Very naturally, she raised her face as he bent his. It was a kiss that began gently in gratitude, then moved with the same naturalness to a burgeoning and mutual hunger. His mouth slid down her throat, tasting the sweetness of her flesh, his tongue seeking the racing pulse that betrayed her own excitement. Her fingers tangled themselves in his dark hair, then drifted to his nape and the hard breadth of his shoulders, searching, probing, exploring with a sureness that moved far beyond her mother's warnings into a new territory for which she had no map, and the only compass was her own feelings.

From a long way away, she heard the fiddler strike up a rollicking jig, followed by the stamp of feet on the deck. Kyle claimed her mouth again, their tongues dancing until Nell wondered if she would melt with sheer pleasure. Against her lips Kyle muttered, "I wish the entire party would disappear. Do you realize the only time you and I have ever been alone was out on the barrens? We've been surrounded by people ever since. I should have kept you out there and made love to you until neither one of us could stand up."

She shivered at his intensity, longing and panic warring in her breast. She'd never made love. How could she know if she'd be able to stand up afterward? But if she told him she was a virgin, he'd want to know why. And how could she tell him about her mother without talking about Anna?

He raised his head, his eyes as dark as the sky. "Tomorrow I can't take you anywhere—I promised Conrad I'd help him caulk his boat. He asked me this afternoon."

Of course he asked you, Nell thought. Because if Kyle was working on Conrad's boat, then Kyle wasn't hanging around Nell. Conrad didn't want Nell and Kyle getting together. It would thwart his plan to get rid of her.

With careful restraint, she asked, "Kyle, are you saying you want to make love to me?"

"Come on, Nell, you're a big girl. You can read the signs."

Feeling her way, she said, "So for you it's just a physical thing?"

"You've got a problem with that?"

"Love them and leave them?" she flung. Conrad had done that to Anna. Is that what she herself wanted?

His fingers dug into her shoulders. "Sounds like you're speaking from experience."

"Sort of." She hesitated. "I'm planning to leave here on Sunday."

"Will you for five minutes forget that darn boat?" he roared.

"Stop yelling at me just because you don't want to answer the question!"

His hold loosened and he gave her a sudden, rueful grin. "You're right. I don't want to. Because I don't know what to say."

"Well, that's truthful at least."

"It is, isn't it? Nell, I don't know what's going on between you and me. I know I can't sleep at night because I want you beside me. I know I've said more about myself in the past five days than I have in the past five years. I know I really like you because you fight right back and you don't let me get away with anything." It was his turn to hesitate. "I also know I don't want you to get on the boat on Sunday and sail out of my life. But beyond that, I don't have a clue.... Although I'll add one more thing and then I'll shut up. Bodies can tell the truth as much as words can. Seems to me your body and mine are giving us a message. Maybe we should just go with it and see what happens."

Her mouth dry, she muttered, "That from a man who's into control?"

"Sex is a very powerful drive," he said with a wry smile.

Wishing she did indeed have some experience she could draw on, Nell said, "We'd better go inside. I bet one of Ellie Jane's cousins is in the kitchen timing how long we've been out here and drawing all the wrong conclusions."

"Don't get on the boat on Sunday, Nell."

It was almost dark. Light streamed from every window in the house; against it, Kyle's body was a dark silhouette, his face in shadow. And Nell's body gave her an answer that might or might not have been truth. Stay, it said. You'll regret it for the rest of your life if you don't find out what this man, this chance-met stranger, means to you. He must mean something. You don't make a habit of melting in men's arms. In fact, you never have before. So stay, Nell. Stay. Kyle made you feel safe, didn't he? Use that safety to launch yourself into the biggest risk of your life.

A week ago, she'd thought that coming to Newfoundland on the strength of some faded words in an old diary had been the biggest risk she'd ever taken. But Kyle was already proving her wrong.

"Say something, for Pete's sake!" Kyle said roughly.

"Look, I'm tied up tomorrow with Conrad. But the next day let's take the dory and go up the lake. Just the two of us."

"To make love?" Nell said with unmistakable hostility.

"To get away from the audience that seems to follow us around. To have fun. To spend some time together." He gentled his tone. "Nell, I'd never force you to do anything you don't want to do. Quite apart from the ethical considerations, which are considerable, what would be the point? No better way to drive you back to Holland, as far as I can see."

"To have fun," she repeated slowly.

"I swear I'll stay five feet away from you the whole time we're gone if that's what it takes."

She took a deep breath and a sizable risk. "I want you, too," she said. "So much that I'm scared I'll do exactly what I want to do—and then regret it afterward."

His breath hissed between his teeth. "I know you want me—I've kissed you after all. Look, let's make a deal. No making love on Friday."

He held out his hand. She took it in hers, the heat of his palm and the strength of his fingers making nonsense of their bargain. "All right," she agreed.

Although that still left Saturday.

After Nell had repaired her makeup in the bathroom, she went downstairs. The kitchen had been restored to some kind of order, and Elsie was standing by the sink chatting to Mary. "Join us, Nell," Elsie called, something in the quality of her smile catching at Nell's throat.

Nell picked up a brownie from one of the trays still out on the table. "Just as well I'll only be coming to one of your parties, Elsie. I'd be as big as a barrel otherwise."

Mary said, "Don't you wave that brownie too close to my nose, Nell. I've been real good and resisted dessert so far. And how d'you know you're only goin' to be at one of Elsie's parties?"

"Sooner or later, I've got to go back to Holland," Nell said with a touch of desperation and felt the words like a death knell. How could a place—and a man—have wrought such a change in her?

"Well, don't be in such an all-fired hurry," Mary said tartly. Then she turned to the other woman. "What d'you think, Elsie? Has Charlie had enough beer that he'll get up and dance?"

"He looked pretty laid-back the last time I saw him."

"That's one of the things I like about Charlie," Mary said. "He doesn't get into the beer very often, but when he does, he's a happy drunk. Maybe I'll go and check him out." She gave a gamine smile. "And introduce this kid of ours to a Newfie reel."

Rubbing at the small of her back, she headed for the deck, where the noise level had risen considerably. "She's a sweetheart," Nell said. "I love to see married couples who stay in love. There was a Canadian couple who lived in the village where I grew up. They were in their forties when I first met them and they used to touch each other all the time. That sounds sappy, I suppose, but it actually wasn't."

"Were your parents in love, Nell?"

Trust Elsie to ask the critical question. "No," Nell replied slowly, "no, I don't think so."

"Looks to me as though Kyle is falling in love with you."

Nell said warmly, "Oh, no, he's not," and blushed.

"Just because I'm seventy-seven years old doesn't mean you can't talk to me about sex," Elsie said with some of Mary's tartness. "Sexual attraction and love aren't always nicely distinguishable, you know. One of them very tidily over here and the other very tidily over there."

The pink in Nell's cheeks deepened. "I've never made love with anyone," she muttered, then grimaced in self-disgust. "I don't know what's happening to me! Ever since I got off the plane in St. John's, it's as though I've turned into someone else. You're the only person in the whole world who knows that, and if you so much as drop a hint to Kyle, I—" she searched for a suitably appropriate threat "—I won't wait for the boat. I'll swim to Caplin Bay."

Unimpressed, Elsie passed Nell a dish towel. "Here, dry these cups. Are you in love with Kyle?"

"I want to go to bed with Kyle."

Elsie laughed. "I like you," she said spontaneously. "I did from the first moment I saw you—felt drawn to you somehow. Kyle's a fine man. If it wasn't for him, Danny wouldn't be alive today."

Nell's ears pricked up. "Kyle didn't tell me that."

"Kyle wouldn't. Closed as a mussel on a rock at low tide is Kyle." Elsie plunked a pile of dessert plates into the suds. "It was after the hostage taking. There were snipers all around the village where they were bivouacked, and one night one of them shot Danny. Kyle ran out into the square and pulled him to safety. That's when he got shot in the knee."

Elsie wasn't a polished storyteller. But Nell's imagination could all too easily fill in the gaps. The darkness wrapped around ruined buildings that stood like jagged, broken teeth. The eerie silence shattered by gunfire. The thud as Danny hit the ground. Kyle's zigzag run toward his friend. The black pools of blood on the greater blackness of the earth. She shivered. "Danny told you?"

"He was home on leave for a while. He thinks the world of Kyle. Said Bosnia nearly drove Kyle out of his mind because there was so little they could do to help." Elsie scrubbed at a fork. "I was real glad to meet Kyle. And if you make him happy, that would be even better."

"Most of the time I make him angry." And the rest of the time he's kissing me as though I'm the only woman in the world.

Elsie shot her a sideways glance that Nell missed because she was rubbing away at a saucer that was already dry. "Danny was like a son to us," Elsie said obliquely. "His parents were our best friends here in the harbor...I still miss Paula, you know, after all these years. Conrad and I pretty well brought Danny up." Her hands slowed. "It's funny how things work out, Nell. I'd have given anything for Paula and Dave not to have drowned. But from that, we had the joy of raising Danny. It was a terrible soreness to me—and sometimes still is—that I couldn't give Conrad his own son. The doctor said it was me, not Conrad. My fault.''

"Fault's an awful word," Nell exclaimed.

"It's my word. Never Conrad's." Elsie's gaze pinioned Nell to the counter. "Conrad's no angel. But I know he loves me, and I love him, too. Don't you be in too big a hurry to get on that boat, Nell. When you're young, you think love can be found for the asking. That it's spread all over the ground like cranberries in a bog. 'Tisn't always so. That's what you learn as you get older.''

The only person who wanted her on the Sunday boat was Conrad, Nell thought grimly. And she couldn't very well share that with Elsie. "I'm not sure I even know what love's about," she said tentatively. "Let alone thinking it grows on every tree and can be mine for the plucking.''

"You see that dryer over there?" Elsie asked.

The dryer was sitting next to the washer; Nell could see nothing out of the ordinary about it. "Yes," she said, puzzled.

"Conrad got me that four years ago. My arthritis was getting as bad as his, and he didn't want me hanging the clothes out in the cold weather. So he ordered that and had it delivered here as a surprise. Now there's people wouldn't get that excited over a dryer. But it wasn't just a dryer. It was Conrad doing his best to look after me.''

Conrad was still doing it. He wanted Nell to vanish so Elsie's peace of mind would be undisturbed. I don't want a man who makes decisions for me, Nell realized with sudden excitement. I want us to make decisions together. And if he were ever unfaithful to me, I'd want to know that, too. No matter how much it hurt.

No secrets.

I do know that much about love.

There was a burst of laughter from the door that led onto the deck, and several of the men came into the kitchen, Kyle among them. The men helped themselves to beer and went back outside. Kyle walked over to the sink; he was favoring his leg. "I just learned I can't dance a reel anymore," he said dryly. "But Samson's going to do a waltz or two in a minute, Nell. Come out on the deck and prop me up, will you?"

The scene in the dark, ruined village vividly in her mind, Nell said, "Elsie told me how you saved Danny's life."

Kyle looked acutely uncomfortable. "Don't make me into some kind of hero."

"You did a very brave thing."

His smile was crooked. "I acted before I thought and I didn't feel brave—I was scared out of my wits."

"That," said Nell, "is real bravery."

He scowled at her. "Are you going to dance with me or not?"

She lifted her elbows level with her shoulders and flexed her muscles. "I've backpacked my way across Newfoundland, so I guess I can prop you up. That was the invitation, wasn't it?"

"Kyle, you've got a thing or two to learn about romance," Elsie said in a militant voice. "You see, Nell, there's something I didn't tell you. When Conrad ordered the dryer, he ordered a big bunch of roses from the flower shop in St. Swithin's, as well. The two of them came together, and the roses probably set him back near as much as the dryer. I never did figure out which one made me cry that day like a newborn babe."

Kyle limped over to the table, extracted a white-petaled daisy from the bouquet that someone had given Elsie, then walked back to Nell. "No roses available," he said, his face lit with laughter, "and the delphini-

ums—which are the color of your eyes, beautiful Nell—
would wreck your hairdo. Then I'd have Mary on my
back along with Elsie.'' He tucked the daisy into her
silky hair, anchoring it with some difficulty, his hands
brushing her cheeks, his nearness making her heart race
as rapidly as the fiddle's beat. Then he swept her a low
bow. "Petronella Cornelia, light of my life, will you
dance with me?''

She sank into a graceful curtsy. "I would be honored
to be your personal support system.''

Kyle glanced at Elsie. "How am I doing?''

"That's a start.''

"Hmmm…'' This time, Kyle came back from the
bouquet with a garish orange marigold, which he proceeded to tuck into the cleavage of Nell's dress.

"Kyle!'' Nell choked and blushed fierily.

He stepped back. "It does rather clash with your
cheeks.''

"It's dripping down my front,'' she wailed.

"Hey, I'm new at this game.'' He cocked his head.
"Samson's playing a waltz. Let's go.''

He took her by the hand. Nell didn't dare look at
Elsie; had she done so, she might have thought that Elsie
looked mightily self-satisfied.

Kyle led Nell to the far corner of the deck and put his
arms around her, pulling her close. "Only a crescent
moon,'' he murmured. "There are limits to my powers.''

Her arm was looped around his neck, her other hand
clasped firmly in his, and every cell in her body came
passionately to life. "I'm not so sure there are,'' she
said.

He began to dance very slowly, making no pretense
that he was going to move from the privacy of their
small square of the deck. His free hand slid to her hips,
drawing them tight against his; his arousal was only too
evident.

Instinctively, she molded herself to him, as pliant in his arms as a wildflower to the wind, and knew her action was both surrender and demand. She whispered into his throat, "If this is what you can do with marigolds and spruce beer, who needs dryers and red roses?"

"Who needs marigolds and spruce beer?" he responded huskily. "All I need is you, Nell."

Deep within her, a trembling started, the first flickers of a fire that could, she knew, engulf her were she to give it rein. She no longer cared. Instead, she gave herself over to a host of delicious and unnerving sensations: the arc of Kyle's ribs, the smooth flow of muscle in his thighs, the soft curl of his hair against his nape. And heat, everywhere heat. She felt naked within her dress, aware of her own body in a way new to her. Aware of her swollen, hard-tipped breasts, of the way her hips were imprinting themselves so wantonly into the jut of his pelvis. Desire, she was discovering, could be both a fierce, compulsive ache that made her long to be truly naked and a molten delight that made her feel fully alive.

Somehow she was almost sure she didn't need to communicate any of this to Kyle; he already knew it. "The marigold doesn't smell so good," she murmured. "Actually, it stinks."

"I'll get rid of it," he said, and slid his fingers across her smooth skin to the valley between her breasts. With deliberate slowness, he drew the flower from her dress and must have felt her quiver like a highly strung racehorse. The marigold fell to the deck. He found her mouth and they clung together in the soft darkness, no longer even swaying to the music.

When Samson swung into a wickedly clever parody of the wedding march, Conrad bellowed, "Break it up, you two!"

Kyle pulled back. Not quite steadily, he said, "We've got an audience again."

They wouldn't have an audience on Friday. Would Kyle stick to his promise to keep five feet away from her the whole day? Would she let him stick to it? Or would she be grabbing him and doing her level—if in-experienced—best to seduce him?

"Conrad sounds cranky," she said.

"It's funny—I get the distinct impression he doesn't like you. Did the two of you start off on the wrong foot?"

"Maybe I bring back memories of the war," she said vaguely. "Oh, good, Samson's playing another waltz. Dance with me, Kyle." With outright provocation, she wrapped her arms around his neck, her breasts straining upward against the hard wall of his chest.

In a strangled voice, Kyle grated, "I'm certainly in no state to walk back into the kitchen."

She knew he wasn't; knew it with every nerve ending in her body and with an artless pride that she could so affect him. But it wasn't love. No matter what Elsie said. Or, for that matter, Anna. It was, quite simply, her own awakening to the power and beauty of passion and sex-uality. To a truth about herself, a truth that had layered itself in secrecy until she met Kyle.

And that, Nell felt, was more than enough.

Love, at this precise moment, seemed totally irrele-vant. One thing at a time, she decided with a kind of dizzy logic, and rubbed her breasts against Kyle's silk shirt until the pounding of his heart and the racing of hers drowned out the lilt of the violin.

It was perhaps as well that the next tune was a reel.

CHAPTER EIGHT

THE following afternoon, Nell found herself walking in the direction of Conrad and Elsie's house. The sun was hidden behind ragged gray clouds that scudded across the sky, and the air was cool. She had slept until midday, for the party hadn't ended until well into the morning, and it had taken her an hour or more to fall asleep after Kyle's good-night kiss on Mary's doorstep.

There hadn't been an audience. It had been a deep, slow and unbearably sensual kiss. Her bed had seemed distressingly empty and her body had cried out for fulfillment. She had slept poorly and had woken to a deep relief that her mother couldn't possibly know the content of her dreams.

Her excuse for the visit was to get Mary's casserole dish, which had been forgotten because Charlie had been rather tipsy last night and had needed guiding homeward. Charlie had been endearingly embarrassed at lunchtime today; although that hadn't affected his appetite.

But Nell didn't want to think about Charlie. She strode along the boardwalk, smiling at the occasional passerby. The real reason for her visit this afternoon was to see Kyle. Even if it meant she had to see Conrad, too.

Conrad's dory was upended on the grass below the deck. Nell wrinkled her nose at the strong smell of tar and called brightly, "Good afternoon."

Kyle was stirring the pot of bubbling tar. He looked up, the wind tossing his hair; his teeth were very white in his tanned face as he smiled at her. "Don't tell me you're only just getting out of bed," he teased. "We've

107

been out here since seven this morning, haven't we, Conrad?''

Conrad shot Nell a disgruntled look and bent to the dory. Nell said naughtily, ''Good afternoon, Conrad. Charlie's got a hangover, too.''

''It's not spruce beer that's wrong with me,'' Conrad growled, and ran a thick strip of tar along the seam between two planks.

Nell put her head to one side like an inquisitive bird. ''Oh? What *is* wrong with you?''

Conrad gave an impatient grunt and Kyle said innocently, ''Did you sleep well, Nell?''

''No,'' she said. ''What about you?''

''Nope.''

He was staring at her as if it had been twelve months since he'd last seen her, not twelve hours. The wind was molding her dark blue shirt to her breasts and her shorts to her legs; Mary had braided her hair, pulling it back from her face in a style that emphasized her cheekbones and the curve of her jaw. The shirt, she knew, made her eyes look very blue. He was standing more than five feet away from her right now, and her whole body felt on fire. ''What time did you really start this morning, Conrad?'' she asked lightly, giving him a second chance. She noticed that Elsie had come out of the door behind the two men. She was wearing one of her voluminous aprons; it billowed like a sail in the wind.

''We started at ten, and the sooner you get out of my hair, the sooner we'll be done.''

In a dangerously quiet voice, Kyle said, ''Conrad, what gets into you whenever Nell's around? I haven't heard you say a civil word to her yet.''

As Conrad dropped the lathe back in the pot and straightened, rubbing at his back, Elsie came around the corner of the deck, still behind him. He said harshly, ''I don't reckon that's any of your business, Kyle. And I'd say it was about time you were leaving us, too.''

In a shocked voice, Elsie cried, ''Conrad!''

Conrad jumped as if he'd been shot. ''What are you doing down here?'' he demanded.

''I came to offer you tea and cookies. What's gotten into you, Conrad Gillis? I've never heard you be so inhospitable!''

Conrad said defensively, ''He told us the first day he was here that he was going out west and it—''

''Shut up, Conrad,'' Kyle snapped.

''Out west?'' Nell repeated blankly.

Conrad gave her a wolfish grin. ''Let the cat out of the bag, did I? Yeah, Kyle's heading for Vancouver Island—as far from Newfoundland as he can get. Mort Harbour's just a pit stop on the way.''

Nell looked Kyle full in the face. ''You never told me that.''

''No,'' he said, ''I never did.''

Conrad grunted, ''There's a fancy clinic out there that's clamoring to get him. His chance to shake the bog from his boots once and for all.''

The mixture of feelings churning inside Nell would have been impossible to label. But it was rage that rose in a froth to the surface. ''Let me tell you something, Kyle Marshall! Not only are you going to stay five feet away from me all day tomorrow—that is, if I decide I still want to go—but I'm not going to open my mouth all day. It's your turn to talk. If you're going to spend time with me, you're going to have to unzip that stiff upper lip of yours and spill the beans.''

''You're mixing your metaphors,'' Kyle said.

But Nell swept on with regal disregard for the niceties of speech. ''I wouldn't even have known you were with the UN forces if I hadn't come to the party last night. Let alone about Danny. The strong-and-silent type does not appeal to me—never has and never will. Have you got that? And to hell with my metaphors!''

Conrad said irritably, ''Stir the tar, Kyle, or it'll thicken up.''

Kyle bent to his task, his T-shirt pulled tight over his back muscles and the long curve of his spine. Nell dragged her eyes away. ''I'm going up to the house for a minute,'' she announced. ''You can tell me when I come back whether you still want to go with me tomorrow, Kyle.''

He looked up, his features a taut mask. ''Yes, I want to go. I'm sorry I didn't tell you, Nell. The time just never seemed right.''

All her other emotions were still in turmoil, and she wasn't yet ready to forgive him. ''It had better be right tomorrow. Or it's going to be one heck of a long day.''

''You be here at eight o'clock tomorrow morning and that's when we'll leave.''

He'd apologized once and he wasn't about to do it again; that was the other message he was giving her. ''All right,'' she said stiffly. ''Elsie, I came to pick up Mary's casserole dish—she needs it for supper.'' Which was stretching the truth a little, but she didn't want to sit through any inquisitions from Elsie and she didn't want to see Kyle again until tomorrow, when she could yell at him without an audience.

Five minutes later, she was on her way back to Mary's, the dish in her haversack. But before she got to the house, she took the path over the hilltop and sat down on the rough granite that overlooked the bay. The sea was sprinkled with whitecaps and the surf splashed against the rocks.

Why should the knowledge that Kyle was going to be living on the other side of the continent upset her so? She, after all, was going back to Holland—Conrad had made that decision for her—and whether Kyle was four thousand or eight thousand miles away from her didn't really make much difference.

She frowned in thought. Somehow Kyle and Newfoundland had become entangled in her mind. In her heart, she amended gloomily. There was nothing very rational about the way she was behaving. Kyle had been born on this bleak, rugged island. His rough-hewn features and his strong body seemed to fit the harshly beautiful landscape that had called to her so imperatively ever since she had first seen it.

It was Newfoundland she was in love with, not Kyle. She'd do well to remember that.

At another level, she was hurt by his reticence. It would have been natural enough for him to mention that he was on his way out west, that this was just a temporary stopover. There had been plenty of opportunities. Instead, he'd skillfully elicited information about her job and her men friends while maintaining an impenetrable silence about himself.

Her thoughts carried her forward. Since seeing the photo of him and Danny last night, she now understood why he had started so violently when the horn had sounded on the coastal boat: for months at a time he'd have been continually alert to mortar fire and mines and snipers' bullets. She also understood the speed of his reactions the very first time she'd met him. Hesitation could have meant death in some of the places he'd been in.

She didn't blame him for not telling her about Danny's rescue, for that would have seemed like boasting. But how could he kiss her with such devastating intimacy and yet not share the basic details of his life over the past several years? How could he keep quiet about where he had lived and about his job?

Her father had never talked about his job. Not that her mother had ever asked; that, after all, was a man's

sphere. But Nell wasn't her mother. Nell abhorred secrets. Perhaps secrecy and intimacy were oppo-
sites…was that what she had come to Newfoundland to
learn? Certainly, the secret she shared with Conrad pre-
cluded any intimacy with him or with Elsie.

She couldn't tell Kyle her secret.

What a hypocrite she was, she thought wretchedly.
Expecting Kyle to bare his soul when she wouldn't bare
her own. If she was smart, she'd phone him and tell him
she wasn't going tomorrow.

Feeling thoroughly unsettled, Nell got up from the
rock and wended her way back to Mary's. She and Mary
went visiting that night, and she got to eat blood pudding
and bottled caribou. While it seemed that everywhere
she looked there was a telephone, she didn't call Kyle,
and ten past eight the next morning found her marching
down Conrad and Elsie's driveway, a picnic lunch in her
haversack, her dark glasses firmly on her nose.

Kyle was out on the deck, pouring gasoline into a
metal container. There was, to Nell's relief, no sign of
either Elsie or Conrad. She waited until Kyle had capped
the container and said composedly, "Good-morning."

He looked up, unsmiling. "You came."

"I said I would."

"Elsie's packed us enough food for a week."

Her smile was nearly natural. "So did Mary."

"One of our appetites will be met at least. The other
one kept me awake half the night."

She said cordially, "You've got all day to tell me
about it, Kyle—because my lips are sealed."

An unwilling grin tugged at his mouth. "Vows of cel-
ibacy and silence. You might as well be in a convent,
Nell."

"I'd want to be the Mother Superior," she quipped.
"I'm glad it's sunny."

"Yeah...the wind could be high on the lake. Have you got a jacket?"

"A jacket, insect repellent, sunscreen, water, fruit, lunch, a camera, binoculars, extra film and a spare pair of socks. I'm all ready for the simple life in the wilderness."

"Nothing much is simple when you're around. You notice I'm not kissing you good-morning?"

She had. "I can't say a monastery looks high on your list, though."

He gave her a leisurely scrutiny from her gleaming chestnut hair, firmly braided, to her businesslike hiking boots. "My thoughts are entirely too earthy. No monk worth his salt would let me in."

His eyes could have been undressing her. She said faintly, "Shall we go?"

Half an hour later, Kyle was at the tiller of Conrad's dory, which was puttering along at the base of a sheer cliff on whose ledges clung tiny spruce trees and lacy ferns. It had taken Nell only a few minutes to see that Kyle was entirely at home in a boat; she gave herself over to the pleasure of being on the water, which sparkled and glinted in the sun. The dory slapped against the waves, rainbows lurking in the spray at the bow. The outboard motor and the swish of water made conversation impossible; for the first time since Conrad had mentioned that Kyle was going out west, Nell felt herself relax.

Copper Lake was seven miles long, bordered by tree-furred hills and waterfalls that clasped the bare rock with long white fingers. Rock slides, which Charlie had told her often followed periods of rain because the layer of earth over the bedrock was so thin, had gouged great channels in the hillsides. Like avalanches made of stone instead of snow, Nell thought with an inward shiver.

When they were nearly at the head of the lake, she

saw a much larger waterfall tumbling down the slope in
a great white swath. "We'll pull in so you can have a
look at it," Kyle yelled, and beached the dory on the
rocky shore.

Nell jumped out and helped him haul the boat away
from the water, the rocks rasping under the keel. She
reached for the hawser just as he did; they were standing
only a foot apart, not five, and she jumped backward
like a child who'd been scalded.

Kyle said harshly, "I said I wouldn't touch you and
I won't."

She was chewing on her lip. "This is so ridiculous,"
she muttered helplessly.

"Is it? Look around you, Nell. Not one other soul
within five miles. I could spread my jacket on the stones.
They're warm from the sun and you'd feel that heat on
your bare back when I covered you with my body....
Tell me you're not thinking along the same lines."

She said shakily, "You put it more poetically than
me. I was just thinking of ripping the shirt from your
back."

"Were you now?" His evident gratification touched
her in that place where no one had ever touched her
before; the desire naked in his face made her weak at
the knees. He said, "I wonder if the day will ever come
when you stop taking me by surprise. If you're in shirt-
ripping mode, I think we should climb to the waterfall."

The bank was very steep. Nell looked upward dubiously. "Is there a path?"

He looped the hawser around a big rock and knotted
it. "You make your own, Nell."

He was speaking metaphorically as much as literally.
"Cute," she said crossly, took a deep breath and started
to climb, using the laurel shrubs and stunted trees as
handholds, her boots latching onto the rough granite.
The mingled scents of wet peat and crowberry filled her

nostrils; lichen crackled underfoot. She saw blue harebells and, in the wet crevices, saxifrage and small pink
orchids.

The roar of the falls was getting louder all the time,
pulling her like a magnet. She went faster, her muscles
limber, stretching to the task. Then the ground flattened,
and she noticed clumps of pitcher plants, their hollow
red leaves designed to drown flies and their round ma-
roon flowers like something a child would construct out
of cardboard.

She looked around to point them out to Kyle. But
Kyle wasn't there. Kyle was several feet below her,
struggling up the slope. With a clenching of her heart,
she saw how he was favoring his left leg. She turned
away so he wouldn't see her watching him, then knelt
to touch one of the pitcher plants. When she heard the
scrunch of his steps close to her, she smiled at him over
her shoulder. "These are weird plants, aren't they?"

He was rubbing his leg. Sweat beaded his forehead,
sweat that came from pain and not exertion, she was
sure. "You didn't have to wait for me," he said nastily.
"I'll get there sooner or later."

"I wasn't—"

"Don't lie to me, Nell! I saw you look back."

She raised her chin. "Kyle, tell me something. Where
are you?"

"What the hell kind of question is that?"

"Just answer it! Where, right now, are you standing?"

"You know where. Near the falls."

"Exactly. You're near the falls. So what if it took you
five minutes longer to get here? Do you think that mat-
ters to me or to the universe?"

"For years I took my body for granted," he snarled.
"Danny and I used to run five miles a day and think
nothing of it. We did rock climbing and rappeling—and
now I can't even get up a goddamned hillside."

Abruptly, he ran his fingers through his windswept hair and let out his breath in a soft whoosh. "And I'm swearing again. Sorry. But do you see, Nell? I was proud of my body. It was fit and it worked, so I scarcely ever thought about it…and now it doesn't work."

She said, speaking clearly over the thunder of the falls, "Kyle, you could easily have been killed when you rescued Danny. But you weren't killed. You're alive. Alive, and standing in the sunshine in a place so beautiful it makes me want to cry." Her voice was shaking. "You're beautiful to me, too. Your body is. Surely you know that? Surely you must know how glad I am that you're here with me, that you didn't bleed to death in the dark in a place so far away?"

He stepped closer, tilting her chin with his hands. Her eyes were swimming with tears and more tears were trickling down her cheeks. "Nell, dearest Nell, don't cry. I can't stand to see you cry." He smoothed her wet skin with exquisite gentleness. "That's the most beautiful thing anyone's ever said to me."

"It is?" she quavered, the tenderness in his face making her heart trip in her breast.

"I don't let people close enough to me to say things like that. But you—you just walk right through those barriers, don't you?"

"I hate secrets!"

"Yet you're a woman of secrets."

Her lashes dropped and she nodded unhappily. "Maybe when you're out west and I'm back in Holland, I'll write you a letter," she mumbled. "I'll tell you why I came here, and then you'll understand."

"Holland and Vancouver Island are a lot more than five feet apart," he noted grimly.

Nell was sick to death of their self-imposed rule; she wanted to throw herself into Kyle's arms and forget about secrets and reality and consequences. Instead, she pulled away from him and said with an attempt at lightness, "I'm not very good at keeping my mouth shut, am I?"

His eyes intent on her tear-stained face, Kyle said, "Do you really want to make love with me, Nell?"

"When I'm with you, I do. You know that as well as I do. But when I'm not with you, I get really frightened." She scowled at him. "Which is pretty smart of me. You are, after all, on your way out west."

He shoved his hands into the pockets of his jeans. "I told you once before that I couldn't have met you at a worse time. I'm thirty-four years old, I've got no job, nowhere I call home, and I'm as fidgety as a caribou in September. This clinic out west, it's a plum of a job. I can't imagine anything more different from where I've been the past eight or nine years."

"And is that what you want?" she demanded. "Comfort and security?"

"I don't know what I want! That's the problem. A problem, I might say, that you've added to considerably." He went on impulsively, "You could come with me, Nell. West, I mean."

She gaped at him. "Don't be silly."

"Why is it silly? You could get lots of translation work out there."

"I want to stay here."

"It's beautiful on the west coast, too. Mountains, glaciers, rain forests, alpine meadows…"

Nell answered this with the absolute truth. "I can't imagine that anywhere else in the world could claim my soul the way this place has."

"So why are you going back to Holland?"

Because Conrad doesn't want me. "No money. No job. That'll do for starters. Every day I stay here I'm losing contracts."

"Newfoundland's no paradise, Nell. High unemploy-

ment, the fishery's belly-up, the climate's the pits. Why
would you want to stay here?''

"You were born here," she said slowly, "and you
left as soon as you could. Whom are you trying to convince, Kyle, me or you?''

With underlying violence, he said, "I left the outport
when I was sixteen because I was desperate to see the
world. Something outside of an isolated village and a
bunch of fishing boats.''

"You've seen more of the world than most people,"
she retorted, trusting her intuition as she warmed to her
argument. "So now are you going to settle into a cozy
little middle-class clinic on an island that looks like an
ad in a tourist magazine? You're worth more than that,
Kyle.''

"You don't think I've earned a respite?''

"Of course you have. But that's not the issue. You'd
be underselling yourself if you go somewhere like that.''

He said furiously, "Why don't you just stick to your
vow of silence?''

"Because I don't want to be a nun—and why don't
you stop yelling?'' she yelled.

He suddenly threw back his head and started to
laugh—great whoops of laughter that drowned out the
sound of the waterfall and brought a reluctant smile to
Nell's lips. "I don't want you to be a nun," he said. "It
would be a terrible waste.''

He took her in his arms and kissed her with a passionate intensity that was like flame to her tinder. She
kissed him back, mouth to mouth, tongue to tongue, bodies melding in the wind and the sun.

It was Kyle who drew back, his chest heaving. "So
much for vows," he said. "Tell me something—are you
protected against a pregnancy?''

She blinked. "No." Why would she be? She'd come
here to find a grandfather, not a lover.

"I deliberately didn't bring anything today. Figured that would keep us honest."

Briefly she closed her eyes. She would never risk what had happened to Anna. "For heaven's sake, let's go and look at these falls," she exclaimed, pivoted and nearly tripped over a rock.

Kyle grabbed her arm. "Careful."

"It's like walking in a minefield here."

"No, Nell," he said quietly, "it's not."

She turned to face him; the lines in his face were bitten deep and her words came out without conscious thought. "Was it very bad, Kyle?"

"It was as bad as it could be," he said in a low voice. "Ugliness, suffering, cruelty, and so little we could do. It nearly drove me mad."

Her heart ached for him. And what could she do? Nothing.

She took his hand and picked her way through the tumbled boulders. The spray was dampening her face; the noise was deafening. Ahead of them, the water plunged twenty feet through the air; Nell clutched Kyle's arm and looked down into a pool that was edged with ferns and ledges of rock. Putting his mouth close to her ear so she could hear him, he said, "Back home, we used to swim in a pool like that."

She craved action. Sex was out, and she'd said more than enough for one day. "Let's do it," she cried. "I've got my swimsuit."

"But I haven't."

She loved it when laughter banished the shadows from his eyes. "I'll turn my back," she said primly, and began to slither her way down the bank, her bottom to the ground in a way that sacrificed dignity for safety and that didn't add to the cleanliness of her jeans. When she reached a little clearing edged with tamaracks, she got to her feet; a series of ledges led into the pool, whose

dark waters eddied and swirled. She smiled at Kyle as
he landed with a thud beside her. "I'll change behind
the tamaracks. Not much point in swearing I won't jump
you, is there? Seeing as I promised I wouldn't say a
word all day."

"Your success rate with vows is exactly nil." He
grinned. "But you can jump me anytime you like,
Petronella Cornelia."

"Do you like me?" she blurted.

His grin widened. "Very much."

"I like you, too." She frowned. "I don't think my
mother liked my father. She respected him and she
needed him and she looked after him. It's something to
do with being able to laugh together, don't you think?"

She looked very serious. Kyle said with the utmost
gravity, "I believe you've just discovered a profound
truth."

She pulled a face at him. "You're making fun of me.
Go skinny-dipping, Kyle. I'm sure the water's cold
enough that neither one of us will be overcome with
passion."

"It'd have to be frozen solid," Kyle said, and dropped
a kiss on the tip of her nose. Nell scuttled behind the
tamaracks.

She took her time getting into her swimsuit, partly
because she was afraid she wouldn't be able to keep her
hands off Kyle were she to come upon him nude, partly
because she needed to think. Kyle belonged in
Newfoundland, she was sure of it. He was a complex
and reticent man who'd seen more of the dark side of
life than was good for him, and whose courage and in-
tegrity she'd come to trust in a way that almost frightened her, so absolute was it. Was she a fool to trust a
man she'd only known for a week? Was she even more
of a fool to think that because she made him laugh, she
was helping him to heal?

The thought of herself in Holland and him on the west coast was more than she could bear.

She wriggled out of her clothes and pulled on her swimsuit. Then she carefully stepped back into the clearing, managing to bang her toes on the granite only twice in the process. For a moment, she couldn't see Kyle and her heart leaped in fear. But then she caught movement on the far side of the pool and relief washed over her.

He had hauled himself up on one of the ledges and was standing, his back to her, under the heavy curtain of spray. The water pummeled his head and shoulders, drenching the narrow hips, taut buttocks and long, lean legs. His head was thrown back, his eyes closed. She stood very still, knowing he wasn't deliberately flaunting his naked body in front of her. This had nothing to do with sex, she came to realize. This was about cleansing. About washing away memories he'd probably never shared with anyone, intolerable memories of wrongs he hadn't been able to right, which had bitten into his soul.

She crept to the edge of the pool and slipped into the water. It was achingly cold. Gasping, she struck away from the rocks, keeping her back to Kyle. Because the other thing she knew was that his act was private. Not hers to share.

For several minutes, Nell swam around the edge of the pool, drifting with the currents, admiring the delicate fronds of the ferns and the lush green of the moss. And all the while, the image of Kyle's body hovered in her mind. Earlier, she had told him she found it beautiful. She would add other words now. Totally masculine, infinitely desirable, as elegantly carved as a statue, yet imbued with all the passions that went with life...

A hand came to rest on her shoulder. She finned her way around, her gaze flying to Kyle's face. He looked peaceful in a way she wasn't sure she'd seen before, as though an intolerable tension had finally loosed its hold.

He said, "You knew I needed to be alone there, didn't you?"

She nodded, droplets of water glittering in her hair and on her sleek, wet shoulders; she didn't quite trust herself to speak.

"You're not only beautiful, intelligent and sexy," he said, smiling, "you're intuitive and sensitive, as well. Thanks, Nell." He leaned over and brushed his lips over hers. "You're cold—we'd better get out."

"This is definitely the Newfoundland version of a cold shower."

"I wouldn't trust it—not with you around. You go first. I'm going to swim for a few minutes."

He wasn't going to jump her, or give her the opportunity to jump him. They had no protection against pregnancy, she told herself sternly, and she couldn't allow history to repeat itself. Her grandmother had had her heart broken by a handsome Canadian who had made love to her and left her. It was a good thing Kyle was being so sensible.

It was a good thing one of them was.

She'd forgotten her towel in the dory. Nell dressed hurriedly, her clothes sticking to her body. Then she started toward the pool to tell Kyle he could get out now.

He hadn't waited. He'd just hauled himself out on a ledge, shaking his hair like a dog before swiping it back from his face. Then he opened his eyes and saw her standing there. To Nell, his lean, scarred body seemed utterly a part of its surroundings, integral to the wild waters, the granite, the sweep of sky. Panic caught her in its grip. Was she in love with the place or with Kyle? How could she separate them? What was happening to her?

He stood still, unselfconscious in his nudity. "When we make love," he said, "I want it to be outdoors. You

do belong here, Nell. I don't know why. I just know you
do.''

She raised her chin. ''You belong here, too.''

''Turn your back,'' he said with a touch of grimness.
''There's a limit to what cold water can do.''

She did so, staring unseeingly across the lake at the
long spine of the hills curving around its shores under
the sun. When we make love, Kyle had said. Not if.

But he hadn't said he belonged here.

If she made love with him, wouldn't she leave a part
of her heart in this wild country forever?

Is that what was meant by a broken heart?

CHAPTER NINE

KYLE and Nell got back to Mort Harbour in time for dinner. They'd gone to the head of the lake where another huge rock slide had torn its way through the trees; they'd surprised a moose on their hike along the beach and spotted a bear high in the hills. They'd kept five feet apart, Nell had said very little, and Kyle had seemed content with her silence.

But as she trudged along the river path back to Elsie and Conrad's, four little words were beating a refrain in Nell's mind: when we make love, when we make love. The counterpoint to that refrain was also in Kyle's voice. Five words, this time. When I go out west, when I go out west. And how, Nell wondered, am I to reconcile the two of them?

Elsie had made a lobster casserole, which she served with vegetables out of her garden and freshly made crusty rolls. Nell ate too much and actually managed to engage Conrad in a conversation about moose—a safe, neutral topic. Elsie produced ice cream and chocolate marshmallow squares for dessert. As she passed the plate to Kyle, Elsie said, "We got a piece of news today from Ellie Jane—she's staying in Drowned Island and she phoned her niece down the road who phoned me. The doctor in St. Swithin's is leaving at the end of August."

Kyle took a square. "Is he?" he said, his tone not encouraging. "Elsie, it's a good thing I don't live here. It's a mystery to me how Conrad stays so thin."

But Elsie wasn't to be deflected. "That means the clinic will be vacant."

"I've got an interview out west in two weeks," Kyle said.

Nell winced. Conrad looked pleased. Elsie did not. "You could do a lot of good in St. Swithin's, Kyle," Elsie persisted. "The clinic there needs a shake-up."

"I can do a lot of good on the west coast, too."

"One more Newfoundlander leaving home," Elsie retorted. "You're not the man I thought you were."

"Now, Elsie," Conrad chided, although a smug smile crossed his face, "remember what he did for our Danny."

"Gratitude's never stopped me from speaking my mind, Conrad. No reason why it should today."

"If the man wants to go out west, that's no crime," Conrad said peaceably. "Nell's going back to Holland, Kyle's heading west—and why shouldn't they? There's nothing here for either one of them."

Nell winced again. "Humph!" Elsie snorted, and poured the tea. Conrad began telling tall tales about the lighthouse keepers along the coast, very entertaining tales that at any other time would have kept Nell spellbound. But not tonight. Why shouldn't he be entertaining? she thought viciously, stabbing her ice cream with her spoon. He was getting his own way. The unwanted granddaughter was going home with her tail between her legs, and her putative suitor was flying in the opposite direction.

She insisted on washing the dishes and then she took her leave. "I'll walk you home," Kyle said.

"No, thanks," Nell said crisply. "I'm going to drop in on Mary's sister on the way. She has a jar of bake apples for me."

She didn't have to stop by Sarah's tonight. But she didn't think she could stand five more minutes of Kyle's company. What had been an irreconcilable dilemma before supper had become occasion for rage during supper.

When we make love, indeed! She wasn't going to become another Anna; that was as clear to her as the sky on a cloudless day. Kyle could behave like Conrad if he liked, but she didn't have to behave like Anna. No, sir. Two gullible women in the family was one too many.

"I'll see you tomorrow, then," Kyle said, his expression unreadable.

"Maybe," Nell replied with a toss of her head.

"You promised me you'd help me with my raspberry jam," Elsie put in. "Tomorrow morning would be just fine."

In a haze of too much spruce beer at Elsie's party, Nell had made some such promise. "All right," she said with bad grace. "Good night, everyone."

It was an effort to close the door quietly behind her. She marched to Sarah's, stayed the shortest time that was polite and sat for over an hour on the rocks behind Mary's, watching the gulls swoop through the sky and listening to the soothing gurgle of the waves on the rocks.

She had never felt so confused in her life.

But then, she realized, she had never done anything so atypical as to leave her job, use up most of her savings and come in search of an unknown grandfather. Not that she'd had a dull life prior to this summer. She'd traveled the width of Europe, learned five languages and dated a lot of men. Any number of women would envy her. But she hadn't let any of the men get close to her. She hadn't wanted to.

Kyle was different.

This didn't seem like a very insightful conclusion. Nell walked over the hill to Mary's and went to bed early. But her sleep was broken by dreams that were an outlandish mixture of the erotic and the terrifying, and in the morning the last thing she felt like doing was making raspberry jam in the house where Kyle was staying.

She set off early. But when she got to the top of Conrad's driveway, he was lopping low-hanging branches from the spruce trees that edged the gravel, and the whine of the chain saw flayed her nerves. When he caught sight of her, he lowered the saw, staring at her. He made no attempt to wave.

Her own gesture of greeting died stillborn. You're a mean-spirited old man, Nell thought furiously, and kept on going past the driveway until she came to a little clearing in the woods that was just visible from the trail. She threw herself down on the grass, gazing at the clouds that were sauntering so aimlessly across the sky. The river breeze was pleasantly cool, Elsie wasn't expecting her yet, and she'd slept very little the night before. Nor did she want yet another useless and upsetting confrontation with Conrad. Her lashes drifted to her cheeks as she was trying to conjure one of the clouds into a flat-bottomed dory with Kyle at the oars.

The cloud was brushing her cheek with cold fingers. Nell's eyes jerked open. In a terror that was a continuation of her dreams, she saw a face poised only feet away from her, a face from a nightmare with hollow eye sockets and the hideous grin of a skull, a malevolent face floating above a filmy cloud of white draperies. She screamed, a piercing scream of pure horror, and pushed herself back on the grass, stumbling to her feet. Tripping over roots, branches whipping at her face, she plunged through the trees toward the trail.

Sobbing with fear, she tripped over a rock in the ditch and landed on her knees on the path, sharp gravel scoring her palms. She scarcely felt the pain. She blundered to her feet, looking back to see if the thing was following her.

Then she heard footsteps on the trail. Someone running. With an incoherent sound of dread, she whirled to flee the other way. But that meant she'd be going away from the village, she thought sickly. Away from people who would help her.

"Nell—stop!"

The voice was as familiar to her as her own, penetrating her terror; and the footsteps, she suddenly realized, had been uneven, as though her pursuer was limping. She leaned against a tree trunk and looked over her shoulder. Kyle was running toward her, a shamble of a run because the slope was steep. Without even thinking, she took three faltering steps toward him and tumbled into his arms.

She was shuddering violently, her heart thudding in her chest as though she'd been running a marathon. Grabbing at his waist, she clung to his shirt as if she'd never let go. From a long way away, she heard him demand, "What happened? I heard you scream. Was it a bear?"

She clutched him all the more tightly, shaking her head. "N-no. It was a face. A horrible face, like a nightmare. Awful, empty eyes. That's when I s-screamed."

He raised her chin, looking at her with concern. "Were you asleep?" She nodded. "It must have been a bad dream, Nell."

"It was real! It woke me." She gave a violent shiver. "Like cold fingers on my skin."

"Sounds like a classic nightmare, sweetheart."

"How can I make you believe it was real?" she gasped. "I didn't dream it!" She released his shirt long enough to show him how badly her hands were trembling. "Dreams don't do that to me. And don't call me sweetheart. Not if you're going out west."

"I don't know where the hell I'm going! Except I do

know one thing. Right now we're going to Elsie's and I'm going to make you a cup of very hot tea.''

"Okay," Nell complied weakly. Even Conrad was preferable to that horrible face, and she knew if she started to giggle she'd never be able to stop. As she and Kyle climbed the slope, she kept her eyes firmly away from the clearing. His arm around her waist was enormously comforting, as was the bulk of his body between her and the woods.

But once they were past the clearing, her brain belatedly began to function. Conrad was the only person who'd seen her go this way, she reflected, her eyes widening. She remembered his silent, baleful stare; she also remembered that the boat left Mort Harbour the next morning and that Conrad wanted her on it. Her footsteps slowing, she said, "The costumes that the mummers wear at Christmastime—are they ugly?"

"Some of them are. When I was a kid, I was scared out of my wits more than once."

"It was Conrad wearing a mask," Nell declared with complete conviction. "Back there in the clearing. I know it was."

"What do you mean? Nell dear, it was a nightmare. Nothing to be ashamed of. I should know. I've had my share of them."

"It was real," she insisted stubbornly. "Conrad wants me on the boat tomorrow and he just applied a little pressure, that's all."

"Nell, you're talking nonsense. Why would Conrad do that?"

She stopped in the middle of the trail, absently brushing away a bee that was circling her head. Conrad no longer deserved the slightest loyalty from her and she was sick to death of secrets. "He's my grandfather," she said.

"*What*?"

"You heard. He's my grandfather. When he was in Holland during the liberation, he and my grandmother, Anna, had an affair. Then his regiment was given orders to leave. She bore his child...who was my mother. I only found out a couple of months ago."

For a moment, Kyle simply stared at her. Then she could see his mind going to work at top speed. "So you came here to find him...that's the secret you've been keeping. Does Elsie know?"

"No. That's why, once I realized she didn't know and that Conrad wanted nothing to do with me, I got on the boat last Wednesday. I really like Elsie. How could I risk hurting her?"

"My God," Kyle said, dazed. "I can see why you wouldn't tell me. Because I'm staying with them. Because my best friend is their surrogate son."

Nell suddenly felt exhausted, every bone in her body aching. "Maybe Elsie would like to have me as a grand-daughter. But then she'd know Conrad had been unfaithful to her. I'm not God, Kyle. I couldn't put her in that position."

"No, you couldn't, could you?" He added gently, "You look as though you need more than a cup of hot tea. Let's go to the house."

"You won't tell her?" Nell added in quick alarm.

"No. Conrad will have to do that."

"He never will and it would serve him right if I'd had a heart attack back there in the woods," she said vindictively. "He'll never tell her, Kyle. He wants the past to stay in the past." She finished unevenly, "Sometimes I think he hates me."

"Come on, you need to sit down. And there's a scrape on your face." Kyle put an arm around her shoulders, she kept hers around his waist, and they walked up the hill together.

"Is your knee all right?" Nell asked in a small voice.

"Haven't covered so much ground so fast since I saw Danny lying in the square," he said cheerfully. "Nearly there."

They went down the driveway toward the house. As they came around the corner, the first person Nell saw was Elsie. Elsie was standing by the shed holding some filmy white draperies over her arm. Nell's heart lurched in her chest. "That's what it was wearing," she said almost incoherently. "Oh, God, it couldn't have been Elsie! Not Elsie—she wouldn't do that to me."

Then she saw Conrad come out of the shed. She and Kyle were closer now; she could see that Conrad looked exceedingly uncomfortable, like a little boy caught red-handed doing mischief. Her expression perplexed, Elsie was saying, "Why did you have one of the mummer costumes out at this time of year? I don't usually keep them in the shed."

Conrad was clearly searching for a reply. Then he caught sight of Kyle and Nell, and his face became a comical blend of dismay, guilt and his normal pugnacity. "Leave it, Elsie," he grunted roughly.

But Kyle interrupted, his voice like a whiplash. "Conrad, did you take that costume up in the woods and deliberately scare Nell? So that she'd get on the boat tomorrow?"

Elsie's jaw dropped. "Conrad! You didn't!"

Conrad jammed his thumbs in his belt, his blue eyes defiant. "Yes, I did."

"I'll have your hide for that," Kyle said, taking a furious step forward, his fists clenched at his sides.

Nell grabbed at him, crying, "He's older than you. You mustn't hit him."

"What did you do that for?" Elsie demanded, and something in her voice stopped Kyle in his tracks and made Conrad look almost cowed.

"I wanted her gone from here," Conrad mumbled.

Elsie put the costume on the ground and her hands on her hips. Her apron had little red flowers on it, and her hair was as white as the draperies at her feet. "You've got a nerve, Conrad Gillis," she announced. "You'd deprive me of my granddaughter without even asking me?"

A robin caroled from the birch trees. The shed door creaked in the breeze. Conrad stood like a man who'd been shot but didn't know enough yet to fall. "You knew?" he croaked.

"I guessed. You like meeting new people, Conrad. You're always pleased to welcome strangers to our door. But not Nell. You were different around her, and I couldn't understand it. I was drawn to her from the start, although I couldn't have told you why. But then at the party the two of you were standing side by side in the kitchen for a few moments, and I suddenly saw a resemblance. That's when I started putting two and two together. And getting four, by the look of you."

Nell held her breath. Husband and wife were facing each other like two old warriors, and for the first time since she had met him she saw real feeling in Conrad's face. Anguish and desperation and a terrible fear. "How could I tell you?" he cried. "I was unfaithful to you, Elsie. To you, who I loved more than life itself."

Elsie said quietly, "I knew you'd been with someone else when you came back from the war. Somehow I just knew."

His jaw dropped. "And you never said anything?"

"I figured you'd tell me when you were ready. I loved you, too, Conrad. And still do."

"All these years I've carried the guilt of it," Conrad said in a cracked voice. "One weekend, that's all, I swear, Elsie. Out of my whole life, that's all."

"I believe you," she said.

"It was four years since I'd seen you, and I hadn't

looked at another woman in all that time. For four years, my buddies were killed all around me. We saw nothing but death and mud and guns and smoke. And then there was Holland. People dancing in the streets, laughing and weeping, and us the heroes. Women and kids kissing us and hugging us—I think everyone went a little crazy.'' His voice broke. "I met Anna at a dance in the camp. God help me, Elsie, she reminded me of you. We made love in a barn in the hay and two days later my unit got orders to move out. I never saw her again. I didn't love her. I hated myself for what I'd done—so I did my level best to forget about it.''

"Until Nell came,'' Elsie added.

"I knew who she was the first moment I clapped eyes on her. I just wanted her gone!'' He straightened his back, and clearly for him no one else existed at that moment but his wife. "Fifty-seven years married, Elsie, and it's the only time I was unfaithful to you.'' Hoarsely, he added, "I'm sorry. More sorry than I can say.''

"I believe you, Conrad,'' Elsie said again. "And I forgive you.''

There were tears in Conrad's eyes. Like a man half his age, he crossed the grass and put his arms around his wife, dropping his cheek to rest on her white hair. "It's more than I deserve,'' he said gruffly. "Elsie, I love you.''

Nell began to edge away, feeling like an intruder in a scene that was intensely private; what she wanted more than anything else was to put her head down and cry her eyes out. But Elsie had turned in Conrad's arms and was looking right at her. "What I would have found harder to forgive, Conrad, is if Nell had left last Wednesday. Don't you see? We have a granddaughter!''

"We?'' Conrad repeated with a careful lack of emphasis. "You mean you're okay with that, Elsie?''

"It makes me so happy I want to burst.'' She tugged

free of Conrad's embrace and walked across the grass toward the young woman standing so still in the sunlight. "That is, if you want to be our granddaughter, Nell. Do you?"

Nell's eyes overflowed. "Oh, yes," she said. "I do. As long as Conrad wants it, too."

Conrad said awkwardly but with obvious sincerity, "Have to say I kinda liked you from the start. You stood right up to me and fought back. I like that. I'm real sorry for all the mean things I said to you. And for that goldarn costume today. I was so scared of Elsie finding out that I went a little crazy."

It was, for Conrad, a massive apology. Nell was crying in earnest now. Elsie hugged her, Conrad hugged her, then Elsie hugged Conrad, and Nell found herself in Kyle's arms. She was still weeping. "I'm d-dripping like Mary's gutters in the rain," she snuffled. "And all because I'm happy."

"No wonder," Kyle said. "You've got yourself a whole new family. I'm sorry I doubted you about the nightmare."

"That's okay—"

Then Conrad broke in. "This calls for a celebration. We'll go to the house and have a drink or two of screech."

Screech was a fiery Newfoundland version of rum. "At nine-thirty in the morning?" Kyle countered, amused.

"Darn right." Awkwardly, Conrad patted Nell on the back, rather as if she were a pony or a heifer that might bolt at any sudden move. "Got to welcome Nell into the family."

"I'm crying again," Nell wailed, and flung her arms around Conrad. "I don't think I've ever been so happy in my whole life."

In the house they toasted Nell and granddaughters in

general; Elsie as grandmother and Conrad as grandfather; Danny as surrogate uncle and Kyle for taking Nell off the coastal boat. The raspberry jam was forgotten. Elsie brought out celery and crackers and her special lobster pâté, which she normally served only at Christmas. And Nell basked in happiness, her face glowing with something that went much deeper than Newfoundland rum.

At a pause in the conversation, Kyle remarked thoughtfully, "So this must be why you love Newfoundland so much, Nell."

"I wasn't expecting to. But from the minute I got off the plane I felt as though I'd come home."

Elsie said wistfully, "I suppose you've got to go back to Holland, though. Your family and your friends and your job are all there. But I'll miss you such a lot."

"I don't really have any family," Nell confessed. "My grandmother never married, I'm an only child, and my parents and Anna are all dead. My job's the problem. You can't just decide you want to stay in another country nowadays. There are all kinds of rules and regulations to follow. To start with, I'm sure you've got to be self-supporting."

Elsie sat up straight. "You mean you'd stay here?"

"Oh, yes," Nell replied, surprised that she had to ask.

"You speak all those languages. You could teach."

"I've never done any teaching," Nell said dubiously.

"Pooh," Elsie scoffed. "You're young and you're smart. You'll learn what you've got to learn."

Conrad took another gulp of rum. "First thing Monday morning, I'll call the immigration people in St. John's. I'm your grandfather, aren't I? What more do they want?"

Nell said in amazement, "You'd do that for me, Conrad?"

"Least I can do," Conrad said.

"Maybe I could stay in Newfoundland because we're related," Nell said with growing excitement.

"Don't see why not."

"That would be wonderful," she exclaimed, and raised her glass one more time. "To Conrad and the immigration department."

Conrad tipped the bottle of screech upside down to get the last drop, and half an hour later Elsie, whose cheeks were as pink as the geraniums in her garden, said with great dignity, "Conrad and I are going upstairs to have a little nap. Screech always does that to me. We'll have a late lunch, and then maybe we could make the jam, Nell."

"I'd love to," Nell answered warmly. Again she hugged them both. "You've made me so happy today— thank you." Then she watched them go upstairs, Conrad's arm around Elsie's waist. Turning back to Kyle, she said, "Let's go outside—I'm too excited for a nap." They settled themselves on the steps of the deck, the breeze toying with Kyle's hair. Nell said, "Now's the time I'm scared I'm dreaming...I can't believe how happy I am."

His gaze lingered on her features. "You look very beautiful," he said. "You've earned your happiness, Nell. It was good of you to put Elsie's interests before your own."

"I didn't really feel I had any choice."

"I think you did. And you chose well."

He was looking at her with such warm approval that Nell was momentarily tongue-tied. "Thanks," she mumbled.

"And it's a darn good thing I got you off that coastal boat on Wednesday."

"Isn't it just?" She chuckled. Then she suddenly sobered. "Kyle, I've got a confession to make."

She looked very serious. He said, "You hate screech."

"It's like drinking dynamite, isn't it? No, it's much worse than that. You know the day you rescued me from the river and brought me here to the house? I set that up. I waited for you on purpose because I didn't know how else to meet Elsie and Conrad." She ducked her head. "I'm truly sorry."

"Those scrapes on your leg—you did them on purpose?" he asked incredulously.

"Oh. Well, not really. The rocks were more treacherous than I expected and I really was in difficulties by the time you saw me. Serves me right for deceiving you."

"No more secrets," he said.

Grateful for his understanding, she said eagerly, "That's it. I hate secrets. I grew up with them, you see."

"Because of Anna?"

So Nell poured out the story of her childhood, of Gertruda who was illegitimate and ashamed of her own existence, and who did her best to transfer that shame to her daughter. "She was terrified of strong emotion and of passion—and why wouldn't she be? As a child far too young to understand, she'd been punished for her mother's passions. There were no red tulips or blue hyacinths in our front garden. No dandelions, either. She used to root them up before they could flower. Just yews and a square of grass that was kept mowed to within an inch of its life."

"Were you young when you left home?"

"Seventeen. I started traveling, staying in different countries and picking up the language—I always had a facility for language. Although I used Holland as a base—Amsterdam for quite a while—I never really settled anywhere. I never wanted to. I was too restless."

"Until you came here."

"Mmm—talk about coming home. If the immigration thing works out, I'll stay here. I'd have to go back to Holland first, of course, and pack up my stuff and say goodbye to my friends and finish a couple of contracts. But that wouldn't take long. In fact, with my computer and a fax machine, I could probably keep some of my European contacts." She gave him a dazzling smile. "And then I could live in Newfoundland. I don't really care where, although it would be nice to be close to Elsie and Conrad."

"You took a big risk in coming here."

Risk. Before she could lose her courage, Nell said rapidly, "There's something else you should know. I suppose because of the way I've been brought up, I've—I've never made love with anyone, Kyle. Scared to, I guess, and why am I telling you all this? It must be the screech."

He looked stunned, as though she'd hit him over the head with the empty bottle. "You're a virgin?"

Her smile was brittle. "Ridiculous, huh?"

"God, Nell…"

She might as well go for broke, she thought. "You're the only man I've ever met who's tempted me to change my status," she admitted with a weak attempt at humor.

He made no attempt to touch her and his dark blue eyes were guarded. "What's so special about me?"

"I don't know, Kyle! How can I explain it? I don't even understand it myself."

He said wryly, "I'm bigger than your mother?"

"That must be it." Her eyes dancing, she ran her eyes over his broad shoulders and long legs. "She was five foot six, so you're definitely bigger. But you make me forget her, as though all her rules were meaningless, and passion—the passion that got Anna into trouble—is the only thing that counts."

"Hell's teeth," Kyle said grimly. "I'm glad we didn't

make love yesterday, Nell. The last thing you need is a pregnancy.''

He had retreated, she realized blankly. Gone somewhere she couldn't follow. ''Shouldn't I have told you?'' she cried. ''I've been so tired of the secrets between us, I just wanted everything out in the open.''

''I had no idea you were a virgin,'' he said in a clipped voice.

For a horrible moment, all the shame her mother had tried so hard to instill in Nell came rushing back. ''It's not an illness,'' she said.

''Of course it isn't. But we're damn well not going to have any kind of a casual affair, Nell. In two weeks, I've got that interview. And remember, you don't want to live on Vancouver Island. You want to live in Newfoundland.''

She felt as though a cold hand was squeezing her heart, milking it of all her happiness. She also felt as though she was being pulled apart. Literally. From one end of the continent to the other. ''I should never have told you.''

''Don't look like that! Dammit, the last thing I want to do today of all days is make you unhappy.''

Risk, she thought, and replied evenly, ''The waterfall healed you. Don't forget that. This whole place would welcome you if you'd let it, because it's your home.'' Then she leaned over, took the taut line of his jaw in her palms and kissed him.

She could feel his resistance, sense the tightness in his shoulders and the rigidity in his throat. With all the skill and sensitivity that she had learned from him, she set out to conquer that resistance. Her fingers gently probed the thick waves of his hair and the hard line of bone behind his ears; she leaned closer, so that her breasts grazed his arm and her thigh rested against his knee. And all the while her lips were stroking his, back and forth with a hypnotic, sensual rhythm, even as the tiny, delicate darts of her tongue were begging him to open to her.

With an inarticulate groan, Kyle seized her in his arms, almost pulling her into his lap in his urgency. There was desperation in the plundering of her mouth, possessiveness in the fierce roaming of her body with his hands, as though he was claiming her in the most primitive of ways, setting his seal on her so that she would never belong to anyone else. And Nell, made bold by his intensity, laid her own claims, her hands imprinting deep within her the curve of bone and ripple of muscle that were the essence of this man.

They almost fell apart. Nell was gasping for breath and the pulse at Kyle's throat was pounding to the beat of his heart. He said with something of the same desperation, "What are we going to *do*, Nell?"

"Stay away from secluded places?"

"Nothing very secluded about Conrad's deck." He drew a ragged breath. "Your eyes look like sapphires, shot with sparks of light. I'm no virgin, Nell, but I'll tell you, I've never in my life lost myself in a woman the way I do with you. One kiss, and I'm gone."

"You don't look very happy about it."

"How the devil can I make love with you and then get on a jet going west? I won't do that, Nell." His smile didn't quite reach his eyes. "We'd better reintroduce the five-foot rule."

"You could make it a thousand feet and it wouldn't make any difference," she said vehemently.

Incredibly, he laughed. "You make me feel like a million dollars, you know that?" He stood up, stretching the tension from his body. "Let's go out back and pick some raspberries."

Nell didn't want to pick raspberries. She wanted to kiss him again. "Raspberries come with thorns and wasps. You should be safe," she said. The raspberries also came with somnolent sunshine, the drowsy hum of bees and the rich ruby red of the berries. Nell stayed on the opposite side of the row from Kyle and diligently filled her container. "I'm going to take these indoors."

He reached between the canes. "Here." The berry in his fingertips was ripe and dripping with juice. Nell took it on her tongue, savoring its sweetness. Kyle said huskily, "The rule hasn't been invented that can keep me from wanting you." Then he carefully wiped the dribble of juice from her chin.

"Maybe we should just forget the rules. They didn't do my mother any good."

"Forgetting them didn't do Anna any good," he retorted. "Bring me out another container, will you, Nell?"

"Yes, Kyle," she said, and stalked indoors.

Elsie and Conrad came out into the garden shortly afterward. They looked very pleased with themselves, Nell thought with an inward quiver of laughter. While Kyle and Conrad stayed outdoors picking, she and Elsie filled two dozen jars with jam, by which time Nell's shirt was sticking to her back and her fingers were stained red. She stayed for supper; Kyle barbecued chicken and Elsie made a salad from the garden.

As she was serving the salad, Elsie said, "I've been thinking. We'll have another party a week from Tuesday night, and that's when we'll tell everyone Nell's our granddaughter."

Conrad choked on a piece of lettuce. "It'll be all over the village if you do that!"

"We'll invite Ellie Jane. That way she'll get her facts straight."

"Ellie Jane wouldn't know a straight fact if it walked into her head-on," Conrad muttered.

As if he hadn't spoken, Elsie went on, "On

Wednesday, you see, Mart Wilkins comes back from the hospital in St. John's, and that'll be a wonderful distraction.'' She looked Conrad in the eye. ''I'm not hiding Nell, Conrad.''

He scratched his head. ''Reckon I can take an evening of Ellie Jane.''

''Good,'' Elsie said. ''That's settled, then. Providing it's okay with you, Nell?''

''It's fine,'' Nell replied, dazed. ''It's more than fine. It's wonderful.''

''You'll still be here, Kyle,'' Elsie said, not phrasing it as a question.

''The interview's the week after that.''

''Maybe they'll cancel it,'' Elsie said. ''Or hire someone else. Have some relish, Nell. It's made with my own zucchini.''

Nell helped herself to the relish. She had two weeks to change Kyle's mind about going out west. Although how she was to achieve that, she had no idea.

He had to stay here. Here with her.

CHAPTER TEN

NELL slept at Mary's on Saturday night and ate her breakfast there the next morning; she spent the rest of the day at Conrad and Elsie's. Kyle wasn't there. He'd gone fishing with three of the boys from the village, Elsie reported. "Probably thought we'd like some time together," she said comfortably. "He's a lovely man, isn't he, dear?"

Nell wasn't about to argue with that. After all, hadn't his absence today filled her with a depth of disappointment that frightened her? But maybe Elsie was right and Kyle was just being tactful in allowing her time alone with her grandparents.

The day went fast. Nell talked a lot; she helped Elsie weed the asparagus bed and helped Conrad repair a tattered green fishing net. She stayed until it was dark and Kyle pushed open the screen door on the porch. In his stocking feet, he walked into the kitchen, where they were sitting around the table, and put his woven basket by the sink. He smiled impartially at all three of them. "Trout for supper tomorrow," he announced. "They started biting around dusk, Conrad. We spent the rest of the day being bitten ourselves." Almost as an afterthought, he added, "Did you have a nice day, Nell?"

"Lovely. And you?"

"Great."

This was the man who had kissed her on the steps of the deck as though there were no tomorrow? "I missed you," Nell said.

She was wearing the blue shirt that made her eyes look purple, eyes that were now turbulent with temper.

Kyle raised his brows. "I thought you'd like a day to yourself with Elsie and Conrad."

"I had a wonderful day with Elsie and Conrad. Don't make decisions for me, Kyle."

"Didn't your mother teach you it's not polite to fight in public?"

"She taught me it wasn't polite to fight."

He laughed. "Petronella Cornelia, I'll love you forever if only you'd put a plate of food in front of me. The three boys I went fishing with devoured anything in the dory that was remotely edible by three o'clock in the afternoon and I'm starving, fly-bitten and in dire need of a shower."

I'll love you forever... "Leftovers," Nell said.

"Five minutes and I'll be down."

He took off upstairs. Conrad started gutting the fish as Nell prepared a generous plate of roast pork and vegetables to be reheated in the microwave that was Elsie's pride and joy. Then Kyle came back into the kitchen, his feet bare, his shirt open, his hair wet. His chest was a tangle of dark hair. Nell pushed the buttons on the microwave and tried to think higher thoughts.

She cut Kyle a generous triangle of blueberry pie and brewed the tea, and the whole time, despite her best efforts to the contrary, she was consumed by an ache of longing. She wanted to make love with him so badly that she was sure it was written all over her; there was no secret about that.

She did her level best to act normally. When Kyle had finished eating, she washed the dishes and said, "I'd better be going. I'll see you all tomorrow."

"I'm going to call immigration first thing," Conrad said.

"Perhaps we could do the second batch of jam," Elsie suggested.

"Sleep well," Kyle said.

He wasn't offering to walk her home. He didn't even kiss her cheek. In fact, as she headed for the door, he'd already turned his back. Nell made her escape and hurried back to Mary's. It was strange, she thought, how things turned out. She'd been granted her wish for grandparents, granted it beyond her expectations. Yet here she was feeling hollow and miserable inside because a man whose existence she hadn't even suspected two weeks ago wouldn't walk her home.

Perhaps she was just greedy, she decided gloomily. She wanted everything. Grandparents and lover.

Lover. She ran the word over her tongue and knew she was ready to take that leap into another new territory, one where she had never traveled before and might well not know the language. She wanted Kyle to teach her that language. But did he want to? Or had her need to unburden herself of all her secrets served only to drive him away?

When she got to Elsie's on Monday morning, Conrad had already phoned the immigration department. "Couldn't understand a word they said," he grumbled. "They're sending me a copy of the regulations. By courier, I told them. None of this first-of-next-week stuff." And his chin jutted pugnaciously.

Conrad would be saltwater to the bureaucratic mind's oil, Nell decided with an inward smile. "Thanks," she said, and dropped a kiss on his snow-white hair.

Elsie didn't have quite enough raspberries for her jam, so Kyle and Nell went out into the garden to pick some more. His attention on the thorny canes, Kyle said, "I didn't walk you home last night for a reason, Nell. I think we should cool it. And I knew damn well that walking you home in the dark would push my willpower beyond its limits."

She was both grateful for his openness and infuriated

by it. "Telling secrets can backfire," she said, and could not for the world have disguised the hurt in her voice. "All I did was drive you away."

He was standing across from her. He said flatly, "I'm honored, flattered and astounded that of all the men you've met, I'm the one you've chosen. But unfortunately, there's another voice going on in my head. And that voice says, 'Don't do it, Kyle. Don't do something you'll regret.'"

Doing her best to understand, Nell said clumsily, "Sex is a big deal for you?"

"Sex?" he repeated irritably. "You and I have moved beyond that particular word, Nell. We're not talking sex here. We're talking making love. A much more complicated issue."

"But it's important to you, isn't it?"

"Of course it is! You're important to me."

Her smile was radiant. "Oh," she said, "I was beginning to wonder if you still wanted me."

His bark of laughter was unamused. "No doubts on that score. But don't you see, Nell? You'd be making love for the first time—so it should be perfect. Absolutely perfect. I've seen so much ugliness the past few years, I couldn't bear it if making love with you was other than beautiful. And," he finished with utter finality, "I won't be Conrad to your Anna."

"Perfect?" she repeated.

"Yeah...not some kind of scuffle in the rocks on the way home to Mary's."

Humbled, Nell said, "You're quite a man, you know that?" Incautiously, she reached for a berry and jabbed her thumb on a thorn. She pulled the thorn out and swiped her thumb on her shirt. "Do you know what? I have a feeling that whenever and wherever we make love, it will be perfect. We don't need the bridal suite in the Ritz. Not us.'' And she gave him another of those radiant smiles.

He put his basket on the ground, walked around the end of the row of canes and kissed her, a long, sensual kiss whose perfection was marred only by Nell's need for more. ''We're going to cool it,'' Kyle said thickly, nibbling at her lower lip, then burying his face in her throat.

''Yes,'' Nell acquiesced, running her hands down the long curve of his spine. She felt a great deal better than she had ten minutes ago. Kyle still wanted her. Kyle thought enough of her that he wanted to give her perfection.

Cool it, Kyle had said. In the next two days, Nell and Kyle didn't make love and they endeavored to behave circumspectly in front of Elsie and Conrad, neither of whom, Nell suspected, was at all deceived. But sexual tension went everywhere with them, sometimes translating itself into a kind of tomfoolery that Nell loved, so different was it from all her mother's repressions.

On Tuesday afternoon, Kyle and Nell went to the village store because Kyle wanted to make a chocolate cake, his one claim, so he told Nell, to culinary fame. The first person the storekeeper introduced them to was Ellie Jane, who was standing watch by the counter. Ellie Jane's face lit up beneath her hennaed hair, and it took all Nell's ingenuity to field her questions, phrased with all the subtlety of a gale-force wind.

Kyle had abandoned her. She finally detached herself from Ellie Jane and located him at the fruit counter. ''You're a coward, Kyle Marshall.''

''You said it. Snipers' bullets are one thing, Ellie Jane another. Did I ever show you how I can juggle?'' He proceeded to toss five oranges in the air and with considerable dexterity keep them there. His tongue was

caught between his teeth in concentration. Nell started
to laugh, a cascade of chuckles that brought Ellie Jane
beetling around the corner of the aisle and caused Kyle
to drop the fruit. He gave Nell a very thorough kiss full
on the mouth. "Ready, sweetheart?"

Ellie Jane's mouth was hanging open. The woman
was practically drooling, Nell observed with another
quiver of laughter. "Ready for what?" she replied with
a pout and a flirtatious wiggle of her hips.

"The chocolate cake, Nell," Kyle lectured sternly.
"That's why we came here, remember?"

She rubbed her breasts against his chest in a move
that could have been accidental and was not, then said,
"We need baking powder. So the cake will rise."

For her ears alone, Kyle muttered, "What happened
to the five-foot rule? It isn't the cake that's rising, my
darling Nell. You'd better walk in front of me to the
counter unless you want me to be the talk of the town."

With a huge effort, Nell kept her eyes above the level
of his belt. She picked up the slabs of baking chocolate
from on top of the oranges, keeping her body between
him and Ellie Jane. She smiled at the gaping woman
with cloying sweetness. "We'll see you again, Ellie
Jane, I'm sure."

"Yes, indeed," Ellie Jane said, and trailed them to
the counter. Nell and Kyle walked back to Conrad's,
holding hands and trading stories of their most outra-
geous exploits in school.

"I think we have a lot in common," Nell remarked,
after chuckling over the very dead cod Kyle had put in
the teacher's wastebasket on the day of a math test for
which he hadn't prepared. "Although I used a dead
mouse that my father had caught in a trap, and it was a
history test. I always hated history."

Kyle stopped in the middle of the boardwalk. "You
make me laugh," he said with sudden discovery.

"That's it! Ever since we've met, you've made me laugh. I think I was in danger of forgetting how, Nell."

With a lump in her throat, Nell said; "It's because I'm happy when I'm with you."

"We can't make love on the goddamned boardwalk," he muttered. "Chocolate cake—Elsie wants it made in time for supper."

When they got home, Conrad was sitting at the kitchen table with a photocopied sheet of paper in front of him. His hair was standing on end and he didn't look happy. "I can't do it!" he exploded as soon as he saw Nell. "It says right here I can only sponsor you if you're under nineteen. What kind of fool-headed rule is that?" Nell swallowed hard and went to stand beside his chair. He poked at the paper. "See? Can you believe it?"

Forcing herself to concentrate, Nell read down the list of those family members who could sponsor an immigrant. Conrad was right. She had to be an orphan, unmarried and under nineteen. *I'm an orphan and I'm not married. Two out of three ain't bad,* she thought sickly, and read the list again. She could be Conrad's wife or fiancée or daughter or mother. But she couldn't be his twenty-six-year-old granddaughter.

She sat down hard in the nearest chair. She'd been naive enough to think that all they had to do was say Conrad was her grandfather and she would be welcomed into the country with open arms. Scowling hugely, Conrad said, "There's another section over here if you don't qualify in the family class. You've got to be independent and I've got to be able to assist you. Whatever that means."

Nell's gaze flicked down the page. To be an investor, she had to have half a million dollars. Scratch that one. To be self-employed, she had to establish her own business. That could take years, she realized in despair.

She heard Conrad say, "I'm gonna phone 'em. Ask

about this independent bit. Why can't they use the
Queen's English?"

Kyle was also reading the document. "Why don't you
let me phone them, Conrad?"

Conrad directed the scowl in Kyle's direction. "I'm
quite capable of taking these guys on."

"That's what I'm afraid of," Kyle said. "It's honey
that catches ants, not vinegar." Conrad made a rude
noise and passed Kyle the phone. Kyle explained the
situation, listened for a few moments, asked a couple of
questions, then said goodbye. He put down the phone.
"Bad news," he said. "Because Nell's mother was illegitimate, Nell has no claim on you as grandfather,
Conrad. The whole family thing is out."

Conrad said something quite unprintable, Elsie paled,
and Nell bit her lip so she wouldn't bawl like a baby.

"You can apply through the regular channels," Kyle
went on, "but it could take a while and you'll have to
go back to Holland."

Nell couldn't bear the look on Elsie's face. Swiftly,
she rose from her chair and put her arms around Elsie.
"I'll come for visits," she said. "As often as I can. We
won't lose touch, I promise, Elsie."

"Not the same as having you here," Elsie returned,
a statement with which Nell could only agree.

"Make us a pot of tea, Elsie," Conrad said, "and
we'll go through this thing with a fine-tooth comb."

The document, however, revealed no simple answers.
Kyle said tightly, "Chocolate cake, that's what we all
need."

Although the cake was rich, moist and delicious, with
icing half an inch thick, it did little to raise anyone's
spirits. "I'll have to go back soon," Nell told them.
"I'm paying rent on my flat while I'm here and I'm not
earning any money. I pretty well cleaned out my savings
account to come here. My father's insurance stopped

when my mother died, you see, and the money from the sale of the house hasn't been cleared by probate yet.''

Conrad started another tirade against the government, a variation on several he'd already made. While Elsie cleaned up the kitchen, Nell read through the document from beginning to end again.

The easiest way for her to stay in Newfoundland was to marry a Newfoundlander. Kyle was a Newfoundlander. But Kyle was determined to live in British Columbia, and besides, she wasn't in love with Kyle. Depressed and frustrated, Nell sat down with the rest of them and watched the news on television. Then she said, ''I'm really tired. I think I'll head back to Mary's.''

Kyle said abruptly, ''I was talking to Mart Wilkins's brother, Joe, the other day, and he said I could borrow his boat any time I wanted—it's a Cape Islander, and I practically grew up on one of those. Why don't you and I go over to Gannet Cove tomorrow, Nell? It'd cheer you up to have an outing.''

She was suddenly sure he hadn't planned this invitation, that it had been forced from him by something else deep within. ''I've heard about the cove,'' she said thoughtfully. ''It's an abandoned outport, isn't it? And very beautiful?''

Kyle said in a voice devoid of emotion, ''We could stay overnight if you took your tent—come back the next morning.''

Nell's heart gave an ungainly flap, like a fledgling bird attempting its first flight. *I want you*, he'd said. *I want our lovemaking to be perfect for you*. He'd said that, too. Was this his way of achieving that aim?

Her mouth dry, she said, ''I'd love to go, Kyle.''

Conrad interjected, ''You'll have to keep an eye on the weather. The marine forecast's talking about high winds the day after tomorrow, and the temperature's supposed to dip.''

"I'll be careful," Kyle promised. "Especially if I have Nell with me."

Nell's heart had settled into a rapid pounding that she was afraid everyone in the room could hear. She desperately longed for him to smile. "What time will we leave?"

"How about after lunch? Joe's finished with the boat by then."

"You come here for lunch, dear," Elsie said, looking very pleased with this turn of events. "And I'll fix the food for your trip."

Kyle pushed back his chair. "I'll walk you home, Nell."

Last night she had longed for him to walk her home; tonight she didn't know what she wanted. She kissed Elsie and Conrad good-night, and in silence she and Kyle walked up the driveway, Kyle striding along as fast as his knee would allow him. As if he were being pursued, Nell thought, and hurried to keep up with him. At the top of the driveway, she grabbed him by the arm. "Are you sure you want to go to Gannet Cove?" she demanded.

"Yes."

To her overly sensitive ears, it was an affirmative that sounded like a negative. "What's going on, Kyle?"

"I can't bear to have you go back to Holland without making love to you. Haven't you figured that out?"

He sounded more angry than loving, and no, she hadn't figured it out. She seethed, "You mean because I'm flying four thousand miles east and you're flying four thousand miles west, you've decided it's safe to take me to bed?"

"I mean exactly what I said—that I'll regret it for the rest of my life if we don't make love, Nell. I'll make sure you don't get pregnant. You don't have to worry about that.''

"I wasn't.''

He took her by the shoulders and kissed her with the overpowering hunger of a starving man. Then he blazed, ''Don't ask me for rational explanations, and if you don't want to make love with me tomorrow, we won't go. I know I'm going against everything I've said, against common sense and caution and all the sane and sensible reasons why we shouldn't make love. Hell, I don't even know what I'm doing.'' He let go of her, stepping back. ''Do you want to go, Nell?'' Then, with an impatient gesture, he grated, ''No, let me rephrase that. Nell, will you make love with me?''

His features were in the shadows and his body looked very big against the dark boughs of the trees; the imprint of his mouth had shot through every nerve that she possessed. Trusting in something stronger than reason, which she couldn't have named, Nell whispered, ''Yes.''

He closed the gap between them. ''You did say yes?''

This time her voice came out much too loudly. ''Yes!''

He took her face between his palms. ''I'll do my best to make you happy, Nell.''

His words were like a vow. Why, then, did she feel so afraid? ''I know you will,'' she said quickly. ''Let's go, Kyle. Mary and Charlie go to bed pretty early and I don't want to disturb them.''

''Twenty-four hours of no one but you and me,'' he said. ''Not even Ellie Jane can spy on us out there.''

Twenty-four hours alone with Kyle. That, Nell felt sure, would be more than enough to turn her life upside down. Was that what she was afraid of?

The Cape Islander was called *Louise* and had a small cabin forward and a big open deck; she was newly painted in white and turquoise, and her engine, according to Kyle, purred like a contented cat. She was hauling a small turquoise dinghy behind her. The weather was still supposed to deteriorate the following day; for now, the sky was a haze of high white clouds, and at the entrance to Mort Harbour, the waves tossed the buoys so that their bells tolled dolefully. Kyle was following the coastline east; the bow wave hissed as it cut through the sea, and in their wake marbled water spread over the swell.

Kyle was standing at the wheel, his legs spread for balance, his hands light on the wooden spokes. He looked supremely happy. Nell, too, was happy. She had woken this morning certain in her heart that to be with Kyle was what she most truly desired. No doubts, no regrets, no fears: they had all died a natural death overnight. There was only this present perfect moment of sea and wind, to be shared with the man who had, uniquely, brought her body to life.

Terns flew past, scissoring the air with pointed wings that had carried them all the way from Antarctica. Long strands of kelp floated in the water like sea serpents. Then Kyle turned the wheel and pointed to starboard. ''Porpoises!''

She saw six or seven sleek black bodies rise in graceful curves out of the water, disappear, then rise again, the wind tearing at the spume of their passage. It was magic, pure magic, and the smile she gave Kyle held something of that magic.

He said roughly, ''Right now I'm exactly where I want to be—and I'm with the only person I can imagine sharing it with.''

Holding to the gunwales, she edged forward, laughing at her clumsiness compared to his agility. She made a lunge for him and wrapped her arms around his waist. ''Me, too,'' she purred.

They kissed. Kyle pulled her back to his chest, put his arms around her and taught her the elements of steering. They saw gannets, chubby red-footed puffins and big dark birds called jaegers that Kyle said were the sharks of the air. They munched on crisp Granny Smith apples and kissed again. The cool salt wind tugged at Kyle's hair as he said quietly, "You don't know how often in the past three years I've pictured myself on the deck of a boat—it's one of the ways I kept my sanity."

"You belong here," she said in deliberate challenge.

"Do I? Or am I just trying to recapture a past that's long gone?" He shrugged his shoulders, the muscles rippling under his shirt. "See that opening in the cliffs? That's Gannet Cove."

The cove was small and exquisitely beautiful, with that edge of sadness that all abandoned settlements wear like a delicate shroud. Some of the houses had years ago been towed away; others had fallen to the ground, tall grass peering through the broken windows. Wildflowers swayed in a gentle breeze; the cliffs sheltered the cove from the cold winds of the ocean.

Kyle anchored the boat and hauled in the dinghy, then they rowed ashore to a pale sand beach where the waves rippled and purled. "Can we camp near the water?" Nell asked eagerly. "I love hearing the sound of the waves."

"Sure. Do you want to put up the tent? I'll go and gather some driftwood for a fire."

The driftwood lay in pale, tangled heaps at the highwater mark. On a slight rise above the beach were two old stone foundations, surrounded by Rugosa rosebushes whose deep pink blooms richly scented the air. Nell drew a long, slow breath, savoring the mingling of salt and sweetness, and found herself watching Kyle as he bent to pick up the driftwood, gazing at the length of his legs in his rubber boots, at the curve of his back and the breadth of his shoulders. Could you make love without being in love? she wondered. *Was* she in love with Kyle?

It was an unanswerable question. She unpacked the tent and swiftly erected it on a smooth patch of grass. Kyle had borrowed two sleeping bags that zippered together. She spread them over the double air mattress, aligned the packs in the vestibule of the tent, then scrambled outside again.

Absorbed in his task, Kyle was building a fireplace from a circle of stones. The driftwood that he'd collected had been worn to a silvery gray by sea and weather. Perhaps that was what a good marriage was like, Nell found herself thinking. A gradual smoothing away of rough edges and flimsy branches until the essence of two people was revealed in all its unadorned simplicity.

She wasn't going to marry Kyle. Eight thousand miles would see to that. But she was going to make love to him. Sleep beside him. Wake up with him in the morning.

Restlessly, she wandered down the beach, picking up driftwood as she went, surprising a little flock of shorebirds that took to the air as one and wheeled in a flash of white over the dark waters of the cove. When her arms were full, she turned back.

For a moment, she couldn't see Kyle. Then she saw him come out of the tent and start toward her. She walked faster, almost running; when he was within twenty feet of her, she dropped the wood on the beach and waited for him, wanting only to be with him and not caring if her desire was written all over her face for him to see.

No secrets. The way she wanted it.

CHAPTER ELEVEN

KYLE'S eyes ranged over Nell's features. Her cheekbones were delicately flushed, her lips parted and her eyes open to him, unshadowed by either coyness or guile. There was pride in her bearing; there was also, implicitly, a surrendering to whatever would happen between them. He said, raising her fingers to his lips, "You shake my heart, Nell, with your beauty and your courage."

Her own heart shook to his words. Then, for a moment, she looked around her. "The place is perfect," she said, her mouth curving in a smile.

"A good beginning, is that what you're saying?" His eyes darkened. "Come to bed with me, Nell. Now."

Hand in hand they walked across the grass to the tent. She crawled in ahead of him, then stopped. Sitting back on her heels, she said raggedly, "You do it every time. Take me utterly by surprise. That's the most romantic thing anyone's ever done for me, Kyle."

He had picked an armful of roses and spread them around the edges of the tent so that their bed was surrounded by the fragrant blossoms. He knelt beside her, watching the play of expressions on her face. "As near as I could get to the Ritz," he said. "I only hope I didn't bring any ants in with them."

She laughed. "Now that wouldn't be romantic."

"I think anywhere you are would be romantic," Kyle said, and reached for the top buttons on her shirt.

His knuckles brushed her breast; she wasn't wearing a bra, and as he spread the fabric apart, he exposed the creamy rise of her breasts, rose tipped, delicately fash-

157

ioned. He eased her free of the shirt, then ran his hands up and down her bare back, drawing her closer so he could kiss her. She swayed into his embrace, tangling her fingers in his hair, then reaching to undo his own shirt.

His body hair was dark, and the flow of muscle over bone entranced her. She laid her hand to his heart, feeling beneath her palm the tight nipple, the warm skin and tangled hair. "It's beating as hard as if you've run all the way from Caplin Bay to St. Swithin's," she murmured.

"I've stopped running. I'm where I want to be."

They embraced, breast to chest, kissing, nibbling, exploring with a growing and irresistible hunger. The pulse pounding in his throat, Kyle pushed her back on the sleeping bag, reaching for the buckle of her jeans. Impatiently, she tugged her hair free of its ribbon so it lay in a chestnut sheet, rippling like water from the way it had been braided.

Nell had wondered if she would be shy of her nakedness in front of Kyle, but discovered only pride as he gazed at the pale sprawl of her limbs, the graceful curves and secret crevices of her body. Then he was pulling at his own jeans, dragging his legs free of them, along with his briefs. Once before, at the waterfall, she had seen him nude, but that had been at a distance, not close and intimate as he was now. Now she could reach out and touch. For now, he was hers.

He was, quite simply, magnificent: a male animal in his prime, lean and—she saw this with a tiny shock of humility—fully aroused. Her body had done that to him, she thought in wonderment. She was female to his male, his mate. Again she was suffused with a sense of rightness. While the future was a mystery, the present was, indeed, perfect. And she knew exactly what she needed to do.

Very gently she ran her hands down his thighs to where the ugly scars blossomed on his knee. Crouching, she kissed the scars, and for a moment laid her cheek against them. "You could so easily have died," she whispered.

"No. Because I was meant to meet you," Kyle said hoarsely, drawing her to lie against him; then, for a long time, he said nothing at all.

His wish, so Kyle had told Nell in the raspberry patch at Conrad's, was to bring her perfection. With single-minded purpose, he now set out to achieve this aim, bringing to her every gift of his mind and body, attuning all his sensitivity to her responses, to her gasps of startled pleasure, her burgeoning hunger and her ardent receptivity. What he might not have expected was the way Nell began, uncertainly at first and then with gathering confidence, to make her own advances.

The heat and strength of Kyle's body first beside her, then covering her, then beneath her, delighted Nell beyond measure. "You're so beautiful," she marveled, straddling him. "I love the way you feel."

Tracing the taut hollow of his belly and the curve of his rib cage, she burrowed her cheek into the rough hair on his chest so she could inhale the clean, masculine scent of his skin. With her lips, she explored the soft skin at his elbows and under his arms; then she allowed herself to be wrapped in the power of his thighs, moaning at the roughness of his tongue on her breast. His fingertips teased her nipples to hardness; his hand slid down her belly to find the soft petals of flesh between her thighs. She twisted to lie on her back, writhing to his touch. As his weight pinioned her to the ground, she tried to pull him in, frantic to be filled by him.

"Wait," Kyle said jaggedly. "Wait, Nell. We've got all the time in the world. And I want you to be ready."

With touching inexperience and undoubted ardor she

moved her hips beneath him and heard him gasp deep in his throat. It was the only encouragement she needed. She took the hardness that was all his need of her and encircled it with her hand. She saw his response in his clenched teeth and blazing eyes; in an upwelling of emotion that she might have labeled love, Nell recognized both her power to pleasure him and her joy in so doing.

"You're like a porpoise," Kyle said huskily, "sleek and graceful and wet, and oh so beautiful."

Trusting her instincts, Nell tried to guide him within her, and again saw his face constrict in that mingling of pain and pleasure that was also consuming her, impelling her toward a conclusion that she could only guess at and that she hungered for with a desperation that made nonsense of caution. His fingers awkward with haste, Kyle dealt with the small foil envelope he had left by the edge of the sleeping bag; then he raised her hips in his hands, and she saw him struggle for gentleness when every impulse in him must have been clamoring for completion.

She arched to take him in, her body taut as a bow, turned to gold by the light coming through the yellow walls of the tent, and felt that first male thrust. Fire shot through her frame. She cried out his name, eclipsed by waves of sensation that were colored the gold of the sun and the red of the fire's heart. A sudden flash of pain made her gasp, and she saw Kyle hesitate, lifting his weight onto his elbows. "Please...don't stop," she begged, and felt another imperious thrust that went far beyond pain into that territory that was new to her. She was filled as she had longed to be filled by this man and this man alone.

Untaught, she matched her rhythms to his, clutching him so strongly that afterward she would find the marks of her nails in his forearms. Clutching him because she was falling, falling into an abyss of sensation that made her cry out his name over and over again until she felt, deep within her, the pulsing that was his own release and heard, in that place to which she had traveled, his own hoarse cry.

He collapsed on top of her. His chest was heaving, his heart pounding as hard as her own. She held him close with all her strength, so happy that she could have wept, so moved that she had no words.

Eventually, against her throat, Kyle murmured, "Nell, are you all right?"

She nodded, ducking her head as he looked at her. "It's so silly," she mumbled. "After what we just did, why should I be shy of showing you that I'm nearly in tears?"

"Did I hurt you?"

She felt his tension; any urge to cry vanished as quickly as it had arisen. "You were perfect," she said with a brilliant smile.

"So were you." He hesitated. "You trusted me, didn't you?"

Surprised, she said, "Of course I did."

He kissed her parted lips. "That was the best gift you could have given me, Nell."

"I told you once before that I feel safe with you...and next time it won't hurt," she said confidently.

"Next time?" Kyle began to laugh, a carefree laugh of pure happiness that made him look young and vital and achingly handsome. "Give me five minutes, sweetheart. Maybe even ten."

She loved it when he called her that. Snuggling into his chest, she whispered, "Thank you, Kyle."

His answer was another kiss, a slow and languorous kiss. It was more than five minutes before they made love again. But not a lot more.

Nell was never to forget the time she and Kyle spent together at Gannet Cove. The intimacy, the laughter, the

fierceness of their coupling and her wild delight in it
were engraved upon her soul. Because she'd made love
with Kyle, she knew that she was changed forever. She
could never go back to the woman she'd been when
she'd jumped out of the turquoise dinghy onto the sand.

Not that it mattered. Kyle was at her side, building a
fire on which they burned hamburgers because they
started kissing and forgot about them; helping her scour
the plates in the sea, then warming her chilled hands
beneath his shirt; laughing at her attempts to straighten
out the sleeping bag after they had wildly and tempes-
tuously come together for the third time. "Why
bother?" he said. "We're only going to mess it up
again."

It was she who had instigated that particular lovemaking with a seductiveness that he had plainly loved
and that she hadn't known she possessed. She muttered,
"I won't be able to climb back in the dinghy tomorrow,
let alone row it."

Her cheeks were still flushed and her eyes very bright.
"I'd like to stay here forever," Kyle said.

Nell felt exactly the same way. But, of course, they
couldn't. "I hate to sound unromantic," she said, "but
if I don't get some sleep soon, I'm going to be yawning
in your face."

"Bored with me already, Nell?"

She ran a finger from his breastbone to his navel.
"What do you think?"

"I think you're wilder than the ocean," he said huskily. "Your breasts are like islands, your hips like a sea
cave, your heels as warm as beach stones." With a hand
that wasn't quite steady, he smoothed her hair back from
her face. "And your eyes shine like the inside of a sea-
shell."

"Oh, Kyle," she responded shakily, "you don't talk
about your feelings often, but when you do, you sure do

a good job.'' She fumbled for words in one of the rare occasions when she wished she could speak her native Dutch. ''I'm so glad I waited to make love until I met you. That it's you I'm with right now.'' She grimaced. ''Not a very fancy speech…sorry.''

''I'm glad you did, too.'' He kissed her on the tip of the nose. ''We could try to go to sleep.''

Nell crawled into the sleeping bag and turned to him as naturally as if they had been sleeping together for months. Curled into his chest, she fell asleep with the suddenness of a tired child.

''Nell…Nell, wake up.''

Nell didn't want to wake up. She wanted to stay where she was, in the sensuous warmth of Kyle's embrace. She looped her thigh over his, burrowed her breasts into his chest and muttered, ''It's too early.''

There was a thread of laughter in his voice. ''Stop that! Nell, we've got to go. The wind's swung around. We're in for a storm and we can't stay here.''

She shifted her head. ''But it's hardly daylight.''

''Six a.m.,'' he said regretfully. ''But I've spent enough time at sea to know we've got to get the hell out of here.''

The sides of the tent were snapping in the wind and she heard the first rap of raindrops on the taut fabric. With sudden, desperate sincerity, she said, ''I don't want to leave!''

''You think I do? But we have to, Nell. A storm could keep us here two or three days. We haven't got enough food. Besides, knowing Conrad, he'd have the Coast Guard, the search and rescue crews and the RCMP out after us. Not to mention the navy.''

She sat up, gazing at him almost as though she was memorizing his features. Then she said, doing her best to accept the inevitable, ''I'll get dressed.''

"Don't look like that," he said harshly. "We'll make love again."

"We will?"

"Of course we will! Here's your jeans. Your boots are in the vestibule. And put on your rain gear. It's going to be cold out on the water."

"Kiss me first," Nell said with the same desperation.

Kyle took her face in his hands and kissed her hard on the mouth. "I'm not going to abandon you the minute we get to shore. Now get moving."

Within ten minutes, they were rowing the dinghy out to the Cape Islander. Nell stashed all their gear forward in the cabin, then helped Kyle haul the dinghy on board and turn it keel up.

"I've got some of those high-energy snacks in my pack," he said, starting the engine before he pulled up the anchor. "Open a couple and pass me one—and keep your head covered. It's going to be cold and wet out there."

The cove was flecked with strands of foam. But the look of the ocean took Nell's breath away, and for the first time she felt fear. "Is it safe?" she asked tremulously as they came around the corner of the cliff and felt the full force of the wind.

"If it wasn't, I wouldn't be bringing you out here. I've been out in a lot worse. We'll be okay, Nell."

She could see he needed his whole concentration to keep on course through the waves, the blown spray and the rain, so she wisely kept to herself her awe of the sea's power and her moments of terror when it seemed to her that *Louise* would be swamped by the swell.

Nell had learned a lot about herself in the past twelve or fourteen hours; now she was learning something rather more pragmatic—that she didn't get seasick. As *Louise* rose to the peaks of the waves and plunged into the troughs, her scuppers awash with water, Nell braced her legs, trying to keep her balance as naturally as Kyle was. He was alternately peering through the cabin's window and keeping his eye on the compass, his hands as light on the wheel as they had been on her body. I'm not going to abandon you, he'd said. She had to trust in that, just as she had entrusted herself to him on the beach of Gannet Cove.

She rummaged in her pack for an apple for Kyle to eat and passed him more of the snacks. It was raining hard now, gusts of rain hitting the sides of the boat like bullets. Shivering, she wished she'd brought another sweater. The cliffs were black with rain, the waves throwing themselves against the bare rock with a ferocity that both exhilarated and terrified her. And again, as she watched Kyle guide the boat through the tumultuous waters with a skill she could only admire, she knew in her heart that this was where he belonged.

With her at his side.

Afraid he would read her thoughts, she turned away from him and, to her infinite relief, glimpsed through a gap in the rain the island guarded by the cliffs of Mort Harbour. Half an hour later, they pulled up at the fishing shack that belonged to Joe Wilkins.

He had been waiting for them. "Proper thing you came back," he pronounced with a knowledgeable glance at the sky. "She's gonna get worse. Nothin' like a westerly. Didn't see Samson's boat anywhere, did you?"

"Didn't see anyone else," Kyle replied. "What's wrong. Are they still out there?"

"Took off to dive for scallops yesterday. They'll be back, sure. Samson's a good hand with a boat. Did you have a good time, missie?"

Nell passed him up her pack and climbed the rungs of the ladder. "Wonderful," she said. "Thanks so much for lending us your boat, Joe."

"Any time."

Kyle paid for the fuel they'd used and the two men shook hands. "Felt good to have the deck of a boat under my boots," Kyle said. "Been a long time. Thanks, Joe." Then Nell and Kyle walked to Mary's because Nell wanted to shower and get changed. At the door, Kyle kissed her and said, "Why don't you catch up on your sleep, Nell? I'll tell Elsie you'll be over this afternoon."

"Are you implying I've got bags under my eyes?"

"Interesting mauve shadows," he teased. "Don't want to give Conrad any more ammunition than we need to."

Suddenly and irrationally, Nell felt afraid, more afraid than she'd been on the heaving deck of Joe's boat. "All right...bye, Kyle."

"I'm not going to run away, Nell!"

"But you're going out west," she retorted. "Oh, Kyle, I don't want to fight now, not when it was so wonderful being with you."

"Then we won't fight." He planted a kiss on her cold lips that was both violent and possessive, then marched away down the path between the bedraggled geraniums. Quickly, Nell went inside.

Nell slept until midafternoon when the repeated shrilling of the telephone woke her. She pulled on her clothes and hurried into the kitchen just as Mary was putting down the receiver. "Samson and his son've been found—three of his brothers went out lookin' for them," she said. "He'd had engine trouble and was nearly on the rocks. They've called Kyle to go to the wharf—they're in bad shape, according to Ellie Jane."

The gale was rattling the eavestrough, smearing the rain against the windowpanes. Nell felt there was nothing she could do to help and knew she should stay out of the way. "I'm going down to the wharf," she declared.

"I'll come with you," Mary said. "Ellie Jane said Charlie's gone to get Kyle on the ATV."

Arm in arm against the force of the wind, the two women struggled down to the wharf. Samson and his son had been carried into the nearest house. Nell stood by helplessly, sensing that she was here because in some strange way these were her people, just as Conrad was her grandfather. Then she heard the sputter of an ATV and watched Kyle slide to the ground from Charlie's vehicle. Kyle saw her immediately. "Come inside," he ordered. "I might need your help."

The events of the next half hour would always be hazy in Nell's memory. What she remembered was Kyle's swift diagnosis of hypothermia; his incisive authority as he organized hot-water bottles and hot soup; his gentleness as he stitched an ugly cut in young Samson's thigh and bathed a scrape on his father's face. "My hands won't work, Doc," Samson muttered.

"The feeling will come back in a while, Samson. Don't worry about it," Kyle said forcefully. "You'll be playing the fiddle again by tomorrow."

The lines in Samson's face relaxed. But Samson's wife, Judy, was standing by, wringing her hands because there was nothing more for her to do. "If you hadn't been here, Doc, they might have died," she quavered, and a general murmur of agreement went around the room.

"They weren't that far gone, Judy."

"Just the same," Judy misted stubbornly, "I'm right glad you were here, and so's my Samson, I can tell. No way the doctor could've come here from St. Swithin's in this storm."

As Kyle looked around the room, Nell realized it was one of the rare times she'd seen him at a loss for words.

Then he looked back at Judy. "I didn't do much," he muttered. "You'd have known what to do."

"Wouldn't have wanted to see Judy stitch up that cut," Judy's sister cracked. "Her seams was always as crooked as an old woman's spine."

In a general release of tension, everyone laughed. Everyone except Kyle, who checked on the boy's progress once again and said nothing. Samson's three brothers were lined up against the wall, drinking tea as dark as wood stain. From Judy, Nell had pieced together the story of the rescue, of two Cape Islanders perilously close to the sharp rocks and the battering waves at the base of the cliff. There was nothing out of the ordinary about the three men, two of whom she remembered dancing with their wives at Elsie's party; yet they were heroes.

Kyle said very little for the next three hours, by which time he pronounced Samson and his son out of danger. "Take it easy the rest of the day. No alcohol or caffeine. Sleep as much as you can and keep warm." To a chorus of thanks he pulled on his jacket. "Coming, Nell?" he asked. "It's okay, Charlie. We'll walk to Conrad's."

Nell followed him out the door. His hands were thrust in his pockets and his forehead furrowed in thought. He set off along the boardwalk as though all the demons of the storm were after him, his head bent before the wind, the rain streaming down the back of his yellow oilskins.

Nell scurried after him. The gale was in their faces; she fought to keep up with him and, from a wisdom whose source was a mystery to her, knew enough not to ask any questions. It wasn't until they were on the dirt track leading to Conrad's that Kyle looked around for her. Buffeted by the wind, she was several feet behind him, her face scrunched against the rain. "Nell, I'm sorry," he exclaimed, "I was thinking about something else and not paying any attention to you. Here, take my arm.''

He threaded her hand through his arm and pulled her close to his body, sheltering her from the worst of the wind. Together they tramped down the driveway and into Elsie's porch. Conrad flung the kitchen door open. ''Samson and the boy—they okay?''

''They're fine,'' Kyle said. ''It'll take them a day or so to recover. But his brothers got to them just in time.''

''That Ellie Jane—trying to tell us they've both got pneumonia,'' Conrad snorted. ''If someone sprains his ankle, she has him with his leg broken in ten places. I've got no patience with that woman at all.''

Nell said pertly, ''You've got no patience period,'' and wrung the water from her braid.

''Now don't you get uppity, miss. One uppity woman's enough for any man.''

Elsie winked at Nell. ''Come in by the stove, dear. What a day! How about some nice fish chowder and tea biscuits fresh out of the oven?''

''I haven't had anything to eat today except those snacks we ate on the boat,'' Nell said in amazement. ''Which was a very long time ago. No wonder I'm hungry.''

Kyle had gone upstairs. Nell helped Elsie set the table and within fifteen minutes they were all seated around the old oak table. The chowder was delicious. Kyle demolished a bowlful in record time and total silence, accepted a second helping and said abruptly, ''I've been thinking.''

''That why you've been sitting there silent as the grave?'' Conrad asked.

Kyle looked around the table, taking his time, and it was on Nell that his gaze came to rest. ''I'm going to stay in Newfoundland,'' he said. ''Tomorrow I'll phone the clinic at St. Swithin's and see if I can arrange an interview for the vacancy there.''

Nell's jaw dropped. ''You won't go out west?''

''No. I'll call them tomorrow, as well, and cancel my appointment.''

Nell was still gaping at him. Conrad drawled, ''Now what made you change your mind, Kyle?''

Kyle ran his fingers through his hair with characteristic impatience. ''I don't even know if I can explain it. Going to Gannet Cove. Being at the wheel of a Cape Islander again. Discovering this morning that I hadn't lost any of the old skills, that I could still make my way home in a storm. That's part of it. And then there was Samson and his son, and the three brothers who risked their lives to find them. All in a day's work to them. No big fuss made, nor will there ever be. But there was a lot of emotion in that little room, and somehow I just knew I was where I was supposed to be.'' He looked back at Nell, a faint smile on his lips. ''You were right all along—I do belong here. I was just too stubborn to see it.''

Almost as though she had to repeat it to believe it, Elsie said, ''So you'll stay and be the doctor at St. Swithin's?''

''If they'll have me.''

''If they don't, they'll have me to reckon with,'' Conrad said irascibly. ''They'll be darn lucky to get you and I'd be the first to tell them so.''

''That means you'll be our doctor, too,'' Elsie said happily. ''As well as at Caplin Bay and Drowned Island. Oh, Kyle, that'll be wonderful! Isn't it wonderful, Nell?''

''Yes,'' Nell answered in a dazed voice.

''The last few months I was overseas I had this image of the mountains,'' Kyle said slowly. ''Thought that was where I needed to go. I'd shaken the dust of

Newfoundland from my feet once. No reason why I'd
want to settle here. But it *is* my home—that's what I've
learned in the past couple of weeks.''

From out of nowhere, Nell heard herself say, ''You
could marry me.''

CHAPTER TWELVE

THERE was an instant's charged silence. Elsie's hand was frozen in midair; Conrad had stopped chewing. Kyle put down his spoon with exaggerated care. "*What* did you say?"

As if on automatic pilot, Nell's tongue emitted the same words, words that had come without thought or volition from a place she hadn't known was hers. "You could marry me—now that you're going to stay here. That way I could stay, too."

"That's what I thought you said."

His mouth became a hard line; his eyes narrowed suspiciously. She added in a rush, knowing it was too late for her to retreat, "According to the immigration regulations, it's the easiest way for me to be accepted into the country. To immigrate, I mean."

"I know what you mean," Kyle snarled. "You'd be using me. For your own convenience."

"We wouldn't actually have to get married," she said with a touch of desperation. "Just engaged."

"Nell, I read the rules, too. They don't look kindly on people who make up fake engagements just so they can stay in the country. Not only would I have to marry you, I'd also have to agree to support you for ten years."

She had forgotten about the fine print. "Oh," she said, "I guess you're right." Then she raised her chin, remembering all that she and Kyle had shared at Gannet Cove. "Would that be so awful? Don't you want me to stay?"

She was sitting directly across from him. He leaned

forward, his fingers gripping the edge of the table. "Tell me one thing—are you in love with me?"

"We've got an audience again," she said weakly.

"Answer the question!"

"No! At least I don't think so...I don't know."

He shoved back his chair, the rasp of wood on linoleum jangling her nerves. "Then this'll make you laugh. Because I'm in love with you. It's one more thing I've learned about myself in the past twenty-four hours— which seems, if you'll forgive me for saying so, to have been going on for a very long time."

"You never told me you were in love with me!"

"I just did."

"But why didn't you tell me at Gannet Cove?" When you were holding me in your arms...when we were joined, man to woman. Although, in deference to their audience, Nell left this thought unspoken, it was all there in her eyes for him to read. And he was an astute man.

"How could I when I was hell-bent on going west and you were hell-bent on living in Newfoundland?"

"Keep your voice down," she said fractiously.

He glared at her and made an obvious effort to modulate his tone. "What difference would it have made if I'd told you?"

Incurably honest, she spluttered, "I—I don't know. Maybe none."

"Right. And in case you're wondering, the answer's no. I won't marry you just so you can stay in Newfoundland. I won't marry you if you're not in love with me. Have you got that?"

"You're yelling again and I should think Ellie Jane's got it all the way down at the wharf."

"What you need to do is sort out the difference between a place and a man. Between this hunk of rock called Newfoundland and me. Whom you were kind enough to call a hunk. You've lumped the two of us together ever since we met, and—''

Stung, Nell protested, ''I haven't!''

''Dammit, you have.''

Driven beyond discretion, she cried, ''You can't make love with a place.''

''And you don't go around using people for your own ends!''

In a single furious gesture, Nell pushed back her own chair. ''I'm sorry I ever opened my mouth and I certainly won't be foolish enough to do so again. Good-*bye*, Kyle Marshall. Have a wonderful life in Newfoundland.'' She stalked to the kitchen door, remembered her manners long enough to add, ''Elsie, I'll call you tomorrow. Sorry to rush off like this. Good night, Conrad,'' and forgot all about politeness as she slammed the door shut behind her.

She thrust her feet into her boots and her arms into her jacket and was out the porch door in a flash. The wind was behind her. Impelled by its rude hands on her back, she ran down the driveway as fast as she could and kept running along the dirt track, not caring if her hair got soaked, not caring if anyone saw her, only wanting to put as much distance as she could between herself and Kyle.

I'm in love with you, I'm in love with you... As her feet hit the boardwalk, she found herself running to the beat of that simple little sentence, boots slapping the wet wood. I'm in love with you, I'm in love with you...

The rain was streaking her face like tears. I don't love you, Kyle Marshall, Nell thought. I never want to see you again.

Driven by a need she couldn't have explained, she clambered up the rock face behind Mary's; it was getting dark and the sensible course would have been to head straight indoors. But Nell didn't feel sensible. At the peak of the hill, she dropped to a crouch. The sea was like a mad thing, flinging itself against its chains, battering itself on the rocks, heaving itself into the air, only to fall back into a seething, chaotic caldron of spray.

It was also utterly impersonal, mocking the storm of emotion in her breast. With a tiny sound of pure distress that the gale whipped away, Nell scrambled to her feet again. She needed people. She needed the warmth of a kitchen and Mary's sympathy—not the ocean's cold, uncaring tumult.

She slid down the hill through the wet grass, and the yellow lights shining through the windows of the unpretentious little houses of Mort Harbour seemed to deride her. She was exiled from them. They had nothing to give her.

In Mary's porch, Nell shucked off her boots, her hands shaking so badly she could barely hang up her jacket. Then she pushed open the door into the kitchen. Mary was sitting by the oil stove, knitting something out of pale green baby wool; Charlie was sitting across from her, working on a crossword puzzle. They looked complete, Nell thought. They didn't need her any more than the sea needed her.

Mary got up. "What's the matter, Nell?"

And Nell, who had made up her mind to go straight to her room, burst into tears. Charlie picked up his paper and, with a look of horror on his face, fled upstairs.

Mary put her arms around Nell and guided her to Charlie's abandoned chair. "Sit down now, and I'll make you a cup of tea. Listen to that, it's the phone. I won't be a minute." Nell sat down, blew her nose and heard Mary say, "Yes, she just got in, Conrad. Do you want to talk to her?...Sure, I'll tell her...Good night." Then she turned to Nell. "That was Conrad. Said he was worried about your getting home and that you're to be sure to go and see him tomorrow."

"Not if Kyle's within ten miles of the house," Nell said viciously.

Mary pushed the kettle over the hottest part of the stove and put tea bags into the pot. "You mad at Kyle?"

Nell wailed, "He's in love with me, Mary."

"That sounds like good news to me. So why're you cryin'?"

"He won't marry me."

Mary frowned. "He always struck me as the kind of fella that if he fell in love with someone, he'd want to marry her. So why won't he marry you?"

"If only he would, I could stay in Newfoundland."

"You're not making a whole lot of sense, you know that?"

Nell swallowed another sob and said very carefully, "I want to stay here. Near Conrad and Elsie. If Kyle married me, I could stay—the immigration laws say so. You see, he's going to apply for the position at St. Swithin's."

"Now that is good news," Mary said. "But if I'm hearin' you right, Nell, you've got the whole thing backward."

"Backward?" Nell repeated, bewildered.

"Yeah…marriage is about love. Not about where you live. You get married because you love someone, and then you decide where you'll hang your hat." She added shrewdly, "Did you tell Kyle he should marry you so's you can stay?" Nell nodded, and Mary laughed. "Bet that didn't go down so good."

"The way he was shouting you could have heard him clear to the wharf," Nell said ruefully.

Mary moved her knitting and sat down. "Now you listen to me. Right now, Charlie works for the store, does odd bits of carpentry and crews in lobster season. If that all falls through, we'd have to leave here. We'd have to move to wherever there's work because we'll have a littl'un to look after. You think it wouldn't tear the heart right out of me to leave here? Course it would—my family's lived in this place for five generations. But I'll go where Charlie goes because I love Charlie more than I love Mort Harbour.''

The very quietness of Mary's voice carried conviction. Nell bit her lip. ''But I don't know if I love Kyle.''

''You sure been actin' like you do.''

''How do you *know* you love Charlie?''

Mary got up and made the tea. Then she sat down again, staring thoughtfully at the gleaming surface of the stove. ''Two ways, I guess,'' she said. ''If he died, part of me would die with him. Not all of me, mind you. But a big part of me. That's one way. The other one's easy. When he's here in the room with me, the room's full. Got everythin' in it that's needed.'' She put her head to one side. ''Don't mistake me. I'm real happy about the baby. But it's Charlie's baby, that's why.''

Moved, Nell whispered, ''That's beautiful, Mary—everything you just said.''

Mary shrugged. ''So how's a room feel to you when Kyle's in it, Nell?''

Nell, who had had no intention of ever telling anyone what had happened yesterday, said, ''We made love at Gannet Cove in a tent. It was as near to heaven as I'm likely to get on this earth and I can't imagine how I could ever make love with anyone else.''

''Then you'd better do some hard thinkin' before you go over to Conrad's place tomorrow.'' She gave Nell a wide grin. ''That's it—no more advice. Want a peanut butter square with your tea?''

''Two,'' Nell said. ''Please.''

She went to bed early, and for a long time lay awake, listening to the rain pummel the windowpanes and the house creak in the wind. Methodically, she went over

her feelings one by one. She liked Kyle. She trusted him.
She'd been intimate with him in ways that had shaken
her soul. Even though she'd known him for only two
weeks, to think of never seeing him again filled her with
a nameless dread. Yet did all that add up to love? The
kind of love on which to build a lifelong marriage as
Elsie and Conrad had? The kind of love that brought
children into the world as Mary and Charlie were doing?

How was she to know? How could she achieve the
certainty that had lit Mary's face with that inner glow?

There was no doubt in Nell's mind about her love
affair with Newfoundland. *Had* she confused Kyle with
a place? Certainly she'd said often enough that he belonged here.

It was hard to admit that an accusation thrown at her
in anger might hold some truth. Gazing into the darkness, Nell struggled to understand her own heart; for
Kyle deserved her honesty.

Kyle also deserved a woman who was head over heels
in love with him and knew it.

Her proposal of marriage, if indeed it had been that,
had been somewhat less than gracious. Face it, Nell, she
told herself unhappily. It had been abrupt, inept and totally unromantic. How could she blame Kyle for accusing her of using him? Were she to marry him simply so
she could stay here, she *would* be using him.

Not that he'd let her. He'd made that clear.

Round and round her thoughts went; but always they
seemed to circle back to the one fact in the midst of her
confusion that was indisputable. Kyle was in love with
her. And each time she reached this point in her cogi-
tations, she found herself smiling into the darkness. A
foolish smile that refused to erase itself. Kyle, hot-
headed, impatient, ardent Kyle, was in love with her.

Last night, she'd slept in his arms after a lovemaking
that had begun with two people and somehow fused

them into one. A lovemaking that had been both passionate and profound. Did *that* mean she was in love with Kyle?

Unfortunately, memories of their lovemaking brought her face-to-face with a second indisputable fact. Try as she might, she didn't know her own heart.

Wishing she had more experience to draw on, Nell pounded her pillow one more time and composed herself for sleep. But it was nearly two in the morning before she drifted off, and even then it was a fitful sleep, disrupted by nightmares. So it was past ten the next morning when she said to Mary with obvious reluctance, "Well, I guess I'd better head over to Conrad's. I wish I had some idea what I'm going to say to Kyle. If I see him. After yesterday, maybe he won't have anything to do with me."

"Tell him you're sorry," Mary suggested.

It was a better beginning than anything Nell had come up with during the long hours of the night. She dressed in her rain gear and set out. The wind had dropped earlier on, although the seas were still high and the rain was pouring down unabated. The boardwalk was slippery and the dirt trail pocked with muddy puddles. All too soon she reached Conrad's driveway.

Panic closed her throat. What if Kyle didn't want to see her again? What if nothing she said made any sense to him? What if in the cold light of morning he was no longer in love with her? She skidded down the driveway and entered the porch. Kyle's oilskins weren't hanging on their hook.

He's gone, she thought in terror, and wondered if such terror was a measure of love. If a room was full when the man you loved was in it, was it not empty when he was absent?

Conrad opened the kitchen door. "Come in out of the wet," he boomed.

"Where's Kyle?"

"Gone for a walk far as I know. Upriver likely, if you didn't meet him on the way."

"Conrad, I have to talk to him. I'll be back in a little while."

"Last night he was as edgy as a horse with colic. This morning he was just plain crabby." Conrad's piercing blue eyes looked straight at her. "Me and Elsie couldn't wish better than the two of you getting hitched," he said gruffly, and kissed her wet cheek. "Good luck to you."

Much heartened, Nell set out again and turned down the trail to the river. Kyle was probably checking on Conrad's dory, bailing the water out of it, she decided, passing the clearing where Conrad had scared her, and then the pool where she had staged her fall into the river what seemed like so long ago. She'd have to tell Kyle the truth: that she didn't know if she loved him with the kind of love that made a good marriage, but that the thought of never seeing him again was more than she could bear.

No secrets.

The water level had risen, the river lapping at the black rocks and dimpled by raindrops. The air smelled richly of spruce needles and peat. Nell was nearly at the turn in the trail when she heard ahead of her a distant rumble like that of thunder. She glanced up at the sky. But, unlike thunder, the noise grew louder and louder until it resembled nothing more than the roaring of a mythical beast, or the pounding of a million buffalo in rout across the prairie—an incomparable noise that filled her with fear.

Her mouth dry, she stood rooted to the middle of the trail, instinctively closing her ears with her fingers in a futile attempt to deaden the noise, longing for it to end and normality to return. This is how the guns must have sounded to Conrad and to Kyle, she thought sickly, and through her fingertips heard water splashing as though a giant were striding up the river. Then, slowly, the racket diminished until, once again, the only sounds were the pinging of the rain on the river and the ripple of waves against the shore. Bigger waves than usual, Nell realized, and began to run.

When she rounded the corner in the trail, she saw what she had subconsciously been expecting: a raw gouge in the hillside. A great cascade of rocks had obliterated the trail and tumbled into the river. Trees were upended as if they were shrubs, tossed like matchsticks into the turbid water. The mud was as slick and wet as new paint.

Kyle. Where was Kyle?

With a whimper of sheer terror, Nell ran forward, frantically searching for the yellow of his oilskins among the snarled boulders, finding only the black of rock and the brown of mud. She screamed his name again and again, praying that he would answer her from beyond the slide. But the cliffs tossed back nothing but the echo of her own voice.

He couldn't be dead. Not Kyle. He couldn't be buried under tons of rock, he who was so vibrantly alive.

She knew instantly that it was beyond her powers to climb the cliff above the slide. She'd have to go for help, get a boat and go by the river. Her breath catching in her throat, she started to run back the way she had come; and with her ran her new knowledge.

She loved Kyle. Of course she did. Now that he might be dead, now that it might be too late, she knew the last secret of her own heart. She was in love with him. Mary had been right. If Kyle were dead, part of Nell herself would also die.

Incoherently praying for his safety, Nell raced along the trail, stumbling over rocks and slipping on the wet peat. She loved Kyle. He had to be safe. He had to be on the other side of the slide, cut off from the houses, but alive.

A stitch was knifing her side by the time she reached Conrad's driveway. She staggered along it, each breath tearing at her lungs, and fell into the porch. Fear stabbing through her, she saw that the hooks where Kyle's oilskins should have hung were still empty. *No*, she screamed inwardly, *no*, and jammed her weight against the kitchen door, bursting into the room.

Elsie was over by the sink and Conrad was sitting at the table. Nell saw them and forgot them in the same instant.

Kyle was standing by the stove. He was dressed in his oilskins and holding a mug in one hand. Kyle. He was alive. He was safe.

Nell grabbed for the doorframe, her cheeks ashen pale, her head whirling and the floor whirling with it, dipping and swaying as if she were on the deck of *Louise*. She muttered, "I never faint," then felt the linoleum rush up to meet her.

Kyle's coffee mug went flying; he caught Nell just before she hit the floor. He thrust her head between her knees and said urgently, "Nell—what's the matter?"

She did not, of course, answer. Somehow, one of her hands had found his wrist. She clasped it as if she were drowning and it was all that could save her, her fingers cold as ice on his skin, her knuckles white as bone. Then she opened her eyes, seeing the blue-and-gray pattern of the linoleum, the wet folds of her rain gear and the yellow oilskins that she had sought for in such terror by the river. Her hand tightened on Kyle's wrist. Slowly, because she felt light-headed and dizzy, she raised her head.

It wasn't a dream. He was real. Alive and breathing, his face only inches from hers, his dark-lashed midnight blue eyes fastened on her, his dark hair falling over his forehead. She whispered, "Kyle, I love you."

His lashes flickered and his jaw tensed. "Don't try to talk yet," he said. "I think you should lie down."

She took a deep, steadying breath. "I love you," she said again, her voice stronger this time. "It wasn't until I thought you were dead that I came to my senses."

"Dead?" he repeated blankly.

"The rock slide," she said.

"What rock slide?"

"Didn't you hear it?"

"Conrad had the radio on."

With a quiver of laughter, Nell said, "This conversation is like the Mad Hatter's tea party." Still holding him by the wrist, she sat up straighter. His breath was fanning her cheek. She rested her other palm along the line of his jaw, where she could feel the roughness of his beard. No ghost that she had ever heard of had a beard. The color coming back to her cheeks because she wasn't dreaming and Kyle was alive, she said, "Conrad told me you'd walked upriver. I went looking for you. I was nearly at the turn in the trail when I heard this awful noise—a rock slide." She gave a reminiscent shudder. "I was screaming your name and you didn't answer and I thought you were dead and that's when I knew that I loved you." Her eyes widened with a new terror. "But maybe you've changed your mind. My asking you to marry me yesterday—that was the dumbest thing I've ever done in my whole life and I wouldn't blame you if you hated me for it. I love you, Kyle. I love you so much, please tell me you haven't changed your mind."

His eyes fired by an emotion that made her pulse quicken, Kyle said, "Dearest Nell, are you accusing me of being in love with you yesterday and not being in love with you today? Why do you think I'm still in my oilskins? Because I was going out to look for you—

Conrad told me where you'd gone.'' Then he added in a voice as rough as granite, "If you'd been ten minutes earlier, *you* could have been killed."

"I suppose you're right—I hadn't thought of that."

He strained her to his chest and said thickly, "How about if we stop chasing each other the length of Mort Harbour and agree that we're in love?"

"Good plan," Nell said.

"And maybe you could let go of my wrist. You're cutting off my circulation."

She looked down and murmured unsteadily, "I had to prove you were real...I was so frightened, Kyle."

"Sweetheart," he said, and kissed her.

With all her newly discovered love and with the expertise she had garnered at Gannet Cove, Nell kissed him back. It was, therefore, a prolonged and thorough kiss from which she emerged with cheeks now healthily flushed. The doorframe was digging into her back, water was trickling down her neck from her hood, and she had a cramp in her calf. She said with deep happiness, "Tell me you love me."

He laughed. "Ordering me around already, Nell?"

"Yes," she said.

"Petronella Cornelia, I love you," he said. "So much so that I think it'll take me a lifetime to convince you." He smiled at her, that rare, sweet smile that she adored. "And now it's my turn. To propose, I mean. Nell, will you marry me?"

"Oh, yes," she said with a dazzling smile, "I will. And Kyle, I'll live with you anywhere. Not just here. Anywhere." Her brow wrinkled in thought. "Our being together is what counts. I see that now. Sure, I really want to live in Newfoundland. But I'd go to the ends of the earth with you."

She had spoken with the kind of intensity that comes

from truth. Kyle said huskily, "I think that rock slide did us one hell of a favor."

"Where *were* you?"

"Down by the river below Conrad's, thinking black thoughts. Then I was in the kitchen, standing by the stove drinking coffee and thinking more black thoughts. Scared out of my mind—if I'm to be honest—to go looking for you. Figured you were going to tell me you were leaving on the next boat. The only plan of action I could come up with was to borrow *Louise* again and kidnap you."

"Any time," Nell said.

Kyle got to his feet, pulling her up with him. "Nell, I love you. I'll love you when I'm as old and cranky as Conrad."

Conrad. She'd forgotten about Conrad. "We've got an audience again," she said. But when she looked around Kyle's shoulder, the kitchen was empty.

"Elsie dragged Conrad into the parlor," Kyle said in amusement. "Much against his will. Do you think we should tell them the good news?"

"In a minute," Nell said, and lifted her face for a kiss.

It was a kiss that brought back very explicit memories of their lovemaking. Against her mouth, Kyle muttered, "We've both got far too many clothes on. Marry me soon, Nell. Or else we'll be migrating to Gannet Cove."

"I said I'd go anywhere with you."

"So you did. Oh, God, Nell, I want you so much, I don't think I'll ever have enough of you." He suddenly raised his head. "Will you want children?"

"I'll want your children," she said. "Absolutely."

"That'll make Conrad and Elsie great-grandparents."

"I think they'll like that, don't you?"

"I think we should tell them we're getting married first," Kyle said.

So they did.

And four days later, at a party that overflowed onto the deck to the tune of Samson's fiddle, Conrad announced to all his friends and relatives that Nell was his and Elsie's beloved granddaughter, that she was engaged to be married to Kyle, and that Kyle was to be the new doctor at St. Swithin's.

It gave Ellie Jane enough to talk about for the next three weeks.

MILLS & BOON®

Next Month's Romances

Each month you can choose from a wide variety of romance novels from Mills & Boon. Below are the new titles to look out for next month from the Presents™ and Enchanted™ series.

Presents™

ONE RECKLESS NIGHT	Sara Craven
MARRIAGE MELTDOWN	Emma Darcy
LONG-DISTANCE MARRIAGE	Sharon Kendrick
THE BRIDE SAID NEVER!	Sandra Marton
SHATTERED ILLUSIONS	Anne Mather
MISTRESS OF THE GROOM	Susan Napier
MICHAEL'S SILENCE	Kathleen O'Brien
FIRST-CLASS SEDUCTION	Lee Wilkinson

Enchanted™

COWBOY TO THE ALTAR	Rosemary Carter
McTAVISH AND TWINS	Trisha David
THE WEDDING ESCAPADE	Kate Denton
WILD AT HEART	Susan Fox
DANIEL AND DAUGHTER	Lucy Gordon
A LOVIN' SPOONFUL	Carolyn Greene
A RECKLESS AFFAIR	Alexandra Scott
FOUND: ONE FATHER	Shannon Waverly

Bureau de Change

How would you like to win a year's supply of Mills & Boon® books? Well you can and they're FREE! Simply complete the competition below and send it to us by 28th February 1998. The first five correct entries picked after the closing date will each win a year's subscription to the Mills & Boon series of their choice. What could be easier?

1.	Lira	Sweden	____
2.	Franc	U.S.A.	____
3.	Krona	Sth. Africa	____
4.	Escudo	Spain	____
5.	Deutschmark	Austria	____
6.	Schilling	Greece	____
7.	Drachma	Japan	____
8.	Dollar	India	____
9.	Rand	Portugal	4
10.	Peseta	Germany	____
11.	Yen	France	____
12.	Rupee	Italy	____

C7H

Please turn over for details of how to enter...

How to enter...

It's that time of year again when most people like to pack their suitcases and head off on holiday to relax. That usually means a visit to the Bureau de Change... Overleaf there are twelve foreign countries and twelve currencies which belong to them but unfortunately they're all in a muddle! All you have to do is match each currency to its country by putting the number of the currency on the line beside the correct country. One of them is done for you! Don't forget to fill in your name and address in the space provided below and pop this page in a envelope (you don't even need a stamp) and post it today. Hurry competition ends 28th February 1998.

Mills & Boon Bureau de Change Competition
FREEPOST, Croydon, Surrey, CR9 3WZ
EIRE readers send competition to PO Box 4546, Dublin 24.

Please tick the series you would like to receive if you are a winner
Presents™ ❏ Enchanted™ ❏ Temptation® ❏
Medical Romance™ ❏ Historical Romance™ ❏

Are you a Reader Service™ Subscriber?   Yes ❏   No ❏

Ms/Mrs/Miss/Mr_____
                                        (BLOCK CAPS PLEASE)

Address_____

_____

_____ Postcode_____
(I am over 18 years of age)

MILLS & BOON®

Back by Popular Demand

Anne Mather

COLLECTOR'S EDITION

Available from September 1997

A collector's edition of favourite titles from one of
Mills & Boon's best-loved romance authors.

Don't miss this wonderful collection of sought-after
titles, now reissued in beautifully matching volumes
and presented as one cherished collection.

Look out next month for:

Title #1   **Jake Howard's Wife**
Title #2   **Scorpions' Dance**

Available wherever Mills & Boon books are sold

DISCOVER
*S*THE ~
ECRETS WITHIN

Riveting and unforgettable -
the Australian saga of the decade!

For Tamara Vandelier, the final reckoning with
her mother is long overdue. Now she has
returned to the family's vineyard estate and
embarked on a destructive course that, in a
final, fatal clash, will reveal the secrets within....

~

Valid only in the UK & Eire against purchases made in retail outlets
and not in conjunction with any Reader Service or other offer.

50ᵖ OFF
COUPON
VALID UNTIL 30/11/1997

EMMA DARCY'S *THE SECRETS WITHIN*

To the Customer: This coupon can be used in part payment for
a copy of Emma Darcy's THE SECRETS WITHIN. Only one coupon
can be used against each copy purchased. Valid only in the UK
& Eire against purchases made in retail outlets and not in
conjunction with any Reader Service or other offer. Please do
not attempt to redeem this coupon against any other product
as refusal to accept may cause embarrassment and delay at the
checkout.
To the Retailer: Harlequin Mills & Boon will redeem this coupon
at face value provided only that it has been taken in part
payment for a copy of Emma Darcy's THE SECRETS WITHIN.
The company reserves the right to refuse payment against
misredeemed coupons. Please submit coupons to: Harlequin
Mills & Boon Ltd. NCH Dept 730, Corby, Northants NN17 1NN.

9 904170 180504

0472 00166